Peter James
HUTCHINSON

Freer's
Stone

novum ◢ pro

www.novum-publishing.co.uk

Climate neutral
Print product
ClimatePartner.com/16547-2201-1002

Believe to Achieve!

Acknowledgements

I'd like to acknowledge my late father, Kevin James Wilkinson, who with patience and love taught me how to spell, read and write.

Additionally my acknowledgement goes out to my mum, Diane Kentish who encouraged me to read and taught me from a young age to put love into everything that I do, with all my heart.

To all the people who know me: "Yes it's finally here ... I hope you enjoy reading this. I have learned that with imagination and patience there's nothing you cannot conquer."

Finally big thanks to the Novum team for making this happen.

CHAPTER 1

Asillian and Jacobi

Asillian was an angel who played it by the book, but looking into *his* eyes made him question his own integrity.

Asillian was an angel of the highest order ... an archangel. And these angels didn't fuck around, he stood just over seven foot tall, and his physique was muscular, lithe and slender. He was extremely agile, his weapon of choice was a katana and his trusty desert eagle, Ebony, which had nickel plating all over it. It also had crosses intricately placed all over the weapon which made it pretty damn lethal to any creature or demon from hell.

His katana blade was that sharp the saying was that if God were to look upon it, he would be cut! The pommel and handle were carved ivory and polished to a creamy white brilliance.

Asillian was not on his own when it came to dealing with the creatures and evil that had spewed up from the bottomless, fiery pit. On his head he wore the helmet of righteousness which could stop a blow from any evildoer's claw or weapon. Across his chest he had armour that too shined blindingly in the sunlight. Across his shins and elbows he had greaves and braces of power.

This angel wasn't just equipped with demon-slaying weapons and armour he was also taught in the way of fighting styles such as tai chi and ju-jitsu. Yes, indeed, pretty nasty stuff if you were on the receiving end.

His companion and mentor was Jacobi. He had no upper armour as he wasn't scared of taking a wound from anyone although he did have sheet metal gloves named Colossuses, because of

7

the way they could crush a demon' s skull like crushing a pizza box under foot. Jacobi was no joke; he stood a foot taller than Asillian and was heavily thick set in his own right. He carried just one weapon that he called the staff of righteousness. This weapon was imbued and bound with holy incantations and blessings of strength.

Not much on a katana blade or a desert eagle, but what the katana blade and Ebony didn't have was the experience of the archangel that wielded it.

And now, trust me that was real power.

Jacobi did have a slight disadvantage though when it came to sight.

The older and much wiser angel had a patch over one eye, where the demon filth Ragnor had snatched it out.

Jacobi was different to Asillian in the way of the arts. He was quite slow but meditation was his weapon; he could resist the call of a wailing banshee.

He could concentrate and slowly but surely enter any mind that he wished, all the while turning their brains to mush within an instance.

Sometimes it would take longer if the victim put up more of a fight but if they were mere runabout creatures such as a lava imp or vampire bat, or something miniscule, you could be sure they would just keel over and die right there and then!

As the pair gentle flew down from Annahiem Asillian wondered what the much older angel was thinking. So he asked as another one of the angel's talents was that they were telepathic and could communicate without speaking. They could also do this with anyone they so wished such as a person or another being.

"It's time we paid Garga a visit," said the much older and wiser angel.

"So it's the badlands then," replied Asillian.

"Yeah," grunted Jacobi.

As the angels touched down on the deserted soil of the badlands, a couple of tumble weeds rolled carelessly on making their endless journey across the landscape ... or what could be recognised as landscape!

As the two angels crushed minute little specks of sand under their boots they made their way towards a little purple painted shack which looked sort of like an oasis.

"This is where the famous Garga ... the notorious Garga, merchant of all things weird and wonderful resides?" asked Asillian.

"Yes," replied Jacobi, "but don't let his appearance fool you, and when we get there let me do the talking!"

As they drew closer to the shack Asillian started to feel as though they were being watched, even though there was no one within a hundred clicks.

As they entered the shack which was made of rotting, sceptic wood.

There was a smell of pure ammonia, a bell rung and a green, slim, angular demon with horns on its head which made it sort of look like a goat, came into view!

From Asillian's point of view the demon seemed to float not walk as it greeted Jacobi.

"Welcome to Garga's shop of the weird and the wonderful ... how may I be of assistance?"

"Knock it off, Garga. You know why we're here ... the seal it has been broken!"

"Broken?"

With this Jacobi grabbed the demon creature and pulled him clean across and over the desk he was behind.

"Don't fuck with me, Garga, not today!!"

"All right, I might know a little bit of information. Ease up, will ya?'"

"Well?"

"Well … there's talk of the anti-Christ … I mean there's whispers from the underworld. Also, well … I can't really say." Garga stuttered.

"How about I knock it out of you then? How's that for a start?"

"Jacobi," Asillian butted in.

"Silence, Asillian this is a matter for me and the plagiarist to work out!"

Jacobi reached to the side of his belt and unhooked a small glass bottle, "Well if you're not going to talk then I suppose I'll accidentally spill a little of this holy water on you?"
    Garga was silent for a split second then just as Jacobi was about to pour the solution onto his skin he cracked.

"Okay, okay, there's going to be an uprising. *He* has found a way around the seventh seal and he's planning on moving up the ranks. First Earth, then Heaven, and well if the seal isn't mended … I'm afraid it's a free for all!" Garga forced a chuckle out. "And there's nothing you can do about it!"

As Asillian unsheathed his sword and held the blade to the plagiarist demon's throat … it sang, anxious to be bathed in the demon's blood.

"You think *He* can stop us?" How about I slay you where you stand and not have a second thought about it?"

Garga winced.

Jacobi shook the demon again. "Where is he and how do we find him?"

"If you'd let me go then I can tell you!"

Jacobi nodded at Asillian and he retracted his katana.

Jacobi reluctantly let the ugly looking demon character go.

"Ye-e-ess," he said and floated over to a shelf, which was on top of a cupboard.

He rummaged around for a couple of seconds then brought out a glass cylindrical tube.

"Ahhh, here it is, the foreseers map, you'll need this to get you where you're going."

"And how is that thing going to help us? We already know where *He* is?"

"Ahhh, but you'll need something mightier than just that flimsy sword or holy handgun, young one!"

"He's right, Asillian. We need this map to show us where the Freer's Stone is."

"Yes-s-s, yes-s-s, you're going to need that Jacobi and this will guide you!"

"Why is it so important, Jacobi?" questioned Asillian.

"Ha!" Jacobi belly laughed that's because it's a magician's map. Holy as well, that's why old Garga here has got it in a tube!"

"Here, let's have a look," Jacobi said pulling the map out and unfurling it.

As he did this Asillian started to cough because of all the dust and mites that came off it.

"And that thing's meant to help us? Huh ... needs burning more like."

"Hush," said the wiser angel, "and watch."

As Asillian looked deeper into the map there appeared to be nothing on it except brown flecks of mud. But then just as Asillian was about to speak the map started to glow, a gold shiny brilliance.

Just then the badlands came up and a pair of tiny looking angel wings appeared.

They floated across the page to where a title of letters started to appear. THE PIT in bold letters came through.

"Whatever does that mean?" uttered Asillian.

"It means that's where we go next, and it's going to get dangerous Asillian."

"Let us go then, master."

"Would be nice if I didn't see you in like a thousand years," Garga hissed.

"Yeah, likewise asshole!" retorted Asillian as they turned on their heels and left the shack.

CHAPTER 2
The Pit

As they pushed through the purple, revolving old saloon doors, a whirling dervish blew up a heap of sand in their faces.

Something hit Asillian hard in the chest instantly knocking him onto the floor.

As this happened Jacobi was swept off of his feet by a tail of some kind.

So the most famous arch angels, Asillian and Jacobi what a pathetic set of fools you both are don't you know the end is coming? Or can you not see it?

As the whirlwind settled a red, imp like creature appeared it could be seen holding a pair of lethal looking daggers.

Asillian got to his feet and readied himself drawing his desert eagle.

Oh came another voice, so you think you're ready to test me do you? Come son of Aron let's see what you've got.

Show yourself demon why do you hide? Are you too scared to cross paths with me? Asillian shouted.

No young one but why toy with me when you can toy with my understudy?

The red imp moved in a blur cutting Asillian across the arm.

"Guess you're mine then speaker of deception?" said Jacobi rising to his feet. He drew his staff of righteousness and stood ready for action.

The invisible demon spoke softly into Jacobi's ear. With that Jacobi jumped and turned a full 180 degrees, but saw nothing.

As Asillian recovered from his cut, the demon imp, ugly looking as he was, smiled devilishly As he did this it flicked out its green, slimy tongue every few seconds tasting the little bit of fear that Asillian had shown.

"My turn now, imp!" Asillian spat.

He fired his desert eagle three times in a row. The bullets just seemed to pass through the imp as sand swirled all around him.

What trickery is this, Asillian thought.

Jacobi remembered that he had his holy water on him and was prepared for the next time the invisible foe would strike!

As Jacobi looked around keeping his wits about him he glimpsed footsteps in the sand. As the footsteps edged closer he pulled the cork out from the bottle of holy water and spread it where the footprints were. Suddenly there was smoke and a screaming ... not much but slightly a clothed green figure could be seen. "I have you now," Jacobi said calmly.

He pulled out his staff of righteousness and brought it down in a very wide arc.

Crunch!

He split the invisible demon's head in two. Nothing but steam and air came out and with that, the demon was no more.

Asillian shot again at the little red imp demon but once again it dodged the holy rounds.

"Use your katana, young one," shouted Jacobi.

Asillian reached to the back of his shoulder, he could hear the blade sing as it wanted to be bathed in demon's blood because that's what it was made for.

"He, he, he," laughed the red demon.

"Come now," screamed Asillian.

The imp swam in and out of Asillian's vision, but the youngish angel tracked the imp with his hawk like eyes, watching his every move. As soon as the imp was about to loop an attack around Asillian's left knee he brought his glistening katana down and around, deflecting the attack.

"Ha!" laughed Asillian, "now we are equal. I will send you from whence you came, monster."

Asillian knew the imp would still be hard to kill as of his speed, but he knew if he let loose with a round from his desert eagle that it would give him a split second chance to slice the demon in two.

With this he let loose a round aiming straight for the imp's head. Just as the mutant, inbred imp brought sand up, Asillian dived on the chance, and with one flap of his wings closed the distance like lightning.

"He, ya," he bellowed, and with one mighty roar he lobbed the demon imp's head clean off, in one fell swoop.

As the corpse of the imp lay on the barren landscape, it charcoaled and turned into flames. It sank into the sand and disappeared leaving a horrid, acrid smell of ammonia.

"Jesus wept! *He* must have sent those, Asillian," said Jacobi.

"Yeah but they were no match for us."

"Ah, yes but they at least slowed us down, and I think that's what *He* wanted."

"So I guess we go to the pit, huh?"

"Yes, the Pit, my closest companion. Come let's hurry," said Jacobi.

With that, the angels both gave a huge beat of their enormous wings and took to the air.

"How do you know where we are going?" Asillian asked.

"Easy little one, we follow the map."
    They encountered a vast canyon which was covered with lichen and other shrubbery and grass-like plants.

As they drew closer to the canyon ... there was a huge opening to a cave.
    "I guess this is where we go in," said Asillian.
    "Yes, the map seems to indicate it so let's go."

They crouched low and brought their wings in so they could fit through the passage quite comfortably. As they entered further there was a smell that was so overpowering, Asillian and Jacobi had to hold their noses.

Holy shit, that's got to be a bad sign. Right, master? A smell like that has got to mean only one thing ... *demons!*

Just keep your wits about you and don't start anything, Asillian. Okay?"

"Okay," replied Asillian.

The two archangels strove further and further into the cave, as it started to descend further and further into what was the unknown. The light was pretty poor and they could hardly see where they were going. Asillian asked the much older and weathered archangel what the place was.

"This is a place you could say where demons gamble with each other."

Asillian was intrigued and asked how and why.

"Well, when demons get bored or are looking to make big bucks, they fight for entertainment in what is known as the Pit."

Just after Jacobi had spoken, Asillian could hear the faint sound of chanting and the beat of drums. "I don't like the sound of this," said Asillian bravely as he did not want his master to see him, as though he were afraid.

"Just stick by me, young one and all will be well," said Jacobi.

As they travelled down into the cave and its recesses, the chanting became louder and clearer.

"*Edu, Edu*" was what Asillian could make out.

The acrid smell got stronger and stronger. Asillian asked "what is that smell?" to Jacobi.
Jacobi hushed Asillian and replied quietly "Demon filth!"

Asillian screwed up his nose because the smell was so overpowering. The cavern widened as they progressed further. "Be on your guard!" directed Jacobi.
As Asillian eyed the terrain that they were in it became clear why the Pit was called exactly that. High on both sides, there were seats carved out of rock, and there exactly in the middle of either sides of the seated stones, was a sort of cage which had sand strewn all over the cave floor.

There were all sorts of demons and ghasts. One had huge frontal horns, others had three or eight eyes, and some were not even as big as Asillian's boot.

In the centre of the ring/cage was a huge ogre type looking creature which had ripped denim jeans and slacks to keep the back of his butt from poking out.

Asillian did not like the look of the demon that was in the ring. He watched as a Medusa type creature was getting its head crushed under the weight of the colossus foot, of the ogre.

Arrgghh! The creature bellowed as it brought its foot down again and again smashing the head of the serpent-like creature's head to a bloody pulp.

Jacobi turned to Asillian immediately. "Listen, young one. I may have to go into the cage with that creature. All I want you to do is find Vanessa the slippery and tell her what we know and see if she can lead us in the right direction. She'll have a price of course. Make a bet with her that that ogre cannot beat me in the cage that should peak her interest a little."

"How will I find her?" Asillian asked intrepidly.

"Just look for smoke and slime," replied Jacobi. "Now go!"

So as Jacobi started to make their way down the rock seats pushing and knocking demons out of the way Asillian started out to find Vanessa the slippery.

When the fight was over, a small rodent-like animal came into the ring. He looked like the narrator of the show. He had a red garment which he pulled up as a shawl but looked less practical and more for comfort. He wasn't very big but his front two teeth were thick and were at least six inches long or more!

"So," it said, "who thinks they can take on the mighty, the titan Edu and survive? C'mon, I know someone out there is wondering will Edu ever be beaten?"

As the rat-like creature pumped up the crowd he caught a glimpse of Jacobi barging past minions and other demons. Some he was passing and others he was just throwing aside like rag dolls.

"Oh look, a lonely archangel all by himself. How quaint," said the rodent.

"Enough. I will challenge this Edu! "You hear, I will challenge this abomination," shouted Jacobi so loudly it reverberated off the cavern walls.

Suddenly a roar went up as the crowd of filth knew there was blood going to be spilt. Either way they were ecstatic as they thought that Jacobi had no chance against their much revered unbeaten champion.

"Okay, we have a challenger. First one to totally obliterate their opponent wins!

CHAPTER 3

Asillian meandered about the cavern looking for any signs of smoke, and just as he was about to give up he spotted and smelled, the distinct smell of ash and brine. For reasons unknown, he knew he was close. Vanessa was an odd looking thing. She had grace but her snake-like body left patches of oozing green slime everywhere.

She had his back to him so she couldn't see what was approaching her from behind. Asillian took this to his advantage and in one clean arc brought out Ebony. Vanessa flinched. "I don't think you know who you're dealing with angel but I only place bets on fighting, nothing else."

"Then tell me, wench where can I find the ones who have broken the seventh seal? Oh, and don't try to play games. I know why they call you Vanessa the slippery"

She turned to Asillian with a tiny hint of attractiveness and said, "How about we put a little wager on how your Jacobi deals with Edu, my fine undefeated champion?"
    Asillian knew this was just a ploy to distract and waste more precious time, which they didn't have.
    "Okay," he agreed and wheeled her round and grasped her neck which was to be honest was quite slippery at this stage. "So, if my brethren succeeds then you give me the lowdown on all the movers and shakers in this whole grand scheme of things, huh?"

"Sure ... sure," she said in her Transylvanian-type accent. "And if Edu wins I want something from you oh zealous one."

"And what would that be?" Asillian asked.

"I would like a kiss from you."

"What ... never, you vile bitch. Why would I ever agree to that?"

"Well, you want the info or not, Asillian. Yes?"

Asillian thought about this for a couple of seconds then weighed up his options. Yes he was stuck and the only way was to agree to the bet. So he did.

"Fuck ... okay, anything wench just no tongues," he said cutting her off.

Silence, now let's watch this battle unfold!

Jacobi meanwhile started to take off his armour leather cladding that would surely have protected him from any projectiles.

Asillian watched and knew that what Jacobi was doing was ditching excess baggage which would in turn make him lightning quick. Well, maybe not lightning quick but it would definitely give him the advantage over the much slower opponent Edu.

"I'm guna smush ya' predd'y head all over this ring, flying man!" said Edu contentedly.

We'll see, he grinned to himself. Jacobi knew that Edu would come charging over within seconds which gave Jacobi just enough time for his terrific plan.

He waited till the last possible second, set himself steady, planted his feet, then tensed up and gave Edu the hardest thump!

Well with that Edu rocked back and forth for a couple of dazing seconds and eventually fell down and took his jeans slacks with him, bum, drool and all.

The arena went ghostly quiet.

All right did you see that shit? I mean he didn't even stand a chance," Asillian whooped in a joyous tone.

"So who's broken the seventh seal?" Jacobi said as he wiped his hands on a bloody rag he found at the side of a waste bin.

CHAPTER 4

Annahiem

Glacial glades swept down from the heavens, there were huge granite faces with low flowing streams. The water was as crystal clear as a champagne glass.

All across the sky there were winged men but these were not men they were angels. Legions and legions of them. Asillian knew this place well it was his own little bit of paradise.

Well it certainly was as God had created it and the rare beauty of it was astounding.

"Why are we here again?" asked the young apprentice.

"We are here because we need to consult the elders, Asillian. I've already explained this to you three times. We don't need the map now we know that we need what is called the Freer's Stone! And that my young one is on mid- Earth

"Oh, okay. But why do we need to consult the elders? Can't we just go to mid-Earth now and look for the Freer's Stone there?

As they came closer to the elders' hall their wing beats came to a billowing steadiness that was both agile and extremely powerful. They settled and went the rest of the way by foot.

The Elders and the Prophecy

Jacobi heaved at the great hall doors. They creaked open with a moan of strife and struggle as if they were in a constant battle with pain.

As Asillian stared in awe at the huge drooping tapestries, he could see battles of old stitched into the fabric. He concentrated as he looked deeper. He saw minions and hell spawn all rising and then he realised it was a great battle, the battle that happened so long ago. Before he was even ordained an angel.

As he awed and was overcome with wonderment at the history and how the tapestry looked, he began slipping behind.

Jacobi noticed this and smiled.

"Are you waiting for all Hell to rise or are you coming, Asillian?"

"Yes, master. I am." As Asillian said this he hurried his step and was soon walking side by side with his companion.

Asillian was a really bright angel but he was very inquisitive at times.

"The tapestries back there, master, what do they show?"

Jacobi looked at the smaller angel and said, "Do you remember the stories of the great and unending battle, the one we almost lost?"

Asillian nodded.

"Well, that is what we have left to remind us what we stand for as an order. And nothing is more important than the balance of Heaven, Earth and Hell, Do you understand?" Jacobi said putting a huge hand on his shoulder ... so nothing is more crucial than retaining the balance, Ya' hear?

Asillian nodded. "Right."

"Come now, the elders are waiting."

Asillian could smell the faintest whiff of camomile and jasmine as they started to get closer to where the elders were situated.

Then he realised why he could smell those scents. In the massive hall there were huge josh sticks burning tirelessly.

Jacobi came to a standstill then he bowed and spoke.

"Elders, I have come at this time of uncertainty and great trouble! I fear the seventh seal has been broken and the prophecy will come true. *He* will return as he once did in the past."
     All twelve of the elders began mumbling and conferring between each other.

Asillian found this very rude but had a sense of prevailing *doom*.

"How do you know this Jacobi, son of Ether?
     We the elders have heard no such information."

Jacobi spoke with more urgency. "I beg you council of the elders hear me now. We got the information from Vanessa, the slippery … and we …"

"Vanessa the slippery," one of the older elders spoke.
     "You get your information from a slippery old wench who writhes and wriggles in the shadows?

"Have you any other proof than just this lack of information from a devilish snake of a thing?"

"No, I am sorry, but …"

"No, buts," boomed the elder, "go about your business and forget about this conversation. We will know if we should be concerned with the likes of *Him*. Go in peace now, Jacobi son of Ether and don't let this trouble you anymore."

"Yes, wise ones," replied Jacobi as he turned on his heels and exited the great hall.

Amelia

Amelia hurried down the side street rushing to get to work. She was never late. Unbeknown to her something was watching.

She exited the side alley and moved across the road towards the underground metro station in London. I hope I catch my train, she thought to herself.

She worryingly rotated the amber-stoned ring she had inherited from her mother when she was just a child.

She negotiated the steps easily because she was deft and light. The train was in ... she would make it to the coffee shop after all.

The bell to the coffee shop door rang as Amelia came in.

"Hey, Ami." was what Shelbi and most of her friends called her.
    "Hey Shelbi, Did you watch the *Match of the Day* last night by any chance?

"No. Missed that one. Was it good? Did Chelsea win?"
    "No, but it was a great game, 3-2 to Arsenal. Saka got a hat trick!

Amelia loved the times when she would go to all the matches with her father.

He would always buy her Cola and a mince onion pie. Neither of her parents were around now. Her father had passed away with cancer and her mother had left because she couldn't cope with all the stress. She just remembered faintly her mother had advised her, never to take that ring off.

Amelia had been working all day and a little into the night. She was ready for her bed.

"Bye," she said to Shelbi. Shelbi was an art student and was only working at the coffee shop to make ends meet or until the time he could afford to start his own business.

The subway was dead; no one to be seen, but Amelia felt as though someone or something was watching her still.

She looked around ... nothing but a loose newspaper page blowing about in the tunnel.

The eyes in the dark

As Amelia went to sit down and wait for the train, her eye line traced the edge of the platform and worked along the yellow warning paint around the edge of the platform.

She looked into the gloom and down the track lines. To her shock and surprise she saw two red slits that looked to be eyes.

She shook her head and looked again ... no nothing there!

The train arrived and she stepped on. There was nobody else on the train just her and the loose newspaper covering on the floor. She was tired and drifted slowly off to sleep.

Suddenly she was on a barren plain with nothing but sand every-where. It was hot ... man it was hot, she thought. She looked off into the distance and saw two figures making their way towards her. At first she thought they were human but as they drew closer she could make out pure white wings raised high on their backs.

She rubbed her eyes and looked again ... Yes, there was no mistaking it these were angels!

Amelia couldn't believe what she was seeing. Then she remembered she wasn't on a barren landscape at all; she was dreaming.

She willed herself to wake up but it didn't come ... she willed again ... *nothing!*

The huge figure on the right was carrying a staff and the other angel who was a little smaller pointed and opened his mouth to speak.

"Where is the Freer's Stone?" said the smaller angel.

"I ... I ... I don't know what you're talking about."

"What are you?" she said trembling all over her body.

"We are the protectors," said the bigger angel.

"And you are dreaming. Wake up, someone is following you."

Amelia woke and was nearly thrown out of her seat by the rocking of the tube train.

As she heard the tube announcer say her stop, she saw the eyes again. She looked again. No, it couldn't be. But yes as she exited the train and walked up towards the steps, the eyes moved and then flashed a very faint yellow.

It wasn't just eyes though. She looked and saw a dog-like shape. It had a huge hairy mane and fangs that were nearly 12 inches long. It was muscular and looked very dangerous.

Amelia raced for the safety of the streets, where there would be traffic and people.

She scaled the stairs in less than a few seconds and was out onto the pavement. Looking behind her she saw that the dog-like animal was giving chase.

She was scared. People were rushing by and she fell against many of them. Then the animal, whatever it was, vanished again.

I'm not dreaming am I, she thought.

All the while she was knocking people out of the way.

She had been certain she had seen the thing following her. She crossed the road with much trepidation.

Asillian comes to the rescue.

"I think if we draw nearer the holder we will make it," Asillian said.

"I hope you're right," replied Jacobi.

"So do I," answered Asillian.

They saw Amelia through the looking glass, but Asillian wasn't assured.

"Do we leave this human to do her own thing and hope she survives?" he asked.

"No, just follow her until she is in danger."

Amelia didn't feel safe walking down the alleyway, but she thought what's the worst that could happen!

At this stage the chimera that was known as an animal with a lion's mane and a dog's body with a long, sharp tail, jumped out from behind a bin and startled Amelia.

"Ahhhh!" screamed Amelia.

Just as the chimera tried to pierce Amelia's heart Asillian chopped it off with his mighty katana. Suddenly the chimera turned into ash and crumbled.

Jacobi stood still and looked impressed.

"Well handled, young one," he uttered.

"Well, you couldn't do much with your staff could you wise one?"

With this he lifted his patch showing cartilage and skin and his eye and said, "Just because you might think I don't see as much as you, doesn't mean I'm blind, Asillian."

Amelia looked stunned and in awe as she managed to say, "Whhoo are you and why are you here?"

Amelia stood back and let them explain themselves.
    "We are an order of angels and we mean you no harm," said Asillian "so don't be alarmed."

We mean you no offence and we want the best for you, even if you regard us badly."

"Where are you from?" said Amelia to the younger angel.

"We are from the domain you call Heaven.
    And you call the place below us Earth? Am I correct?" he said with deep confidence.

Amelia looked at the younger angel with nothing but pure astonishment, as Asillian was very handsome and had a very strong jawbone and longish, blond hair down to his shoulders. She felt this attraction but she could not explain why.

"Who's your friend then?" she managed to say after all the ogling she'd done.

"This is Jekobe and don't worry he doesn't bite!"

With that Jekobe let out a chesty but loud laugh which only lasted for a couple of seconds.

Asillian was taken aback by this as he had never heard Jacobi laugh in all of the millennia of knowing him.

"Hello, Amelia. I guess you don't know why we are here, and I'm guessing you don't know where the freer stone is, do you?"

Freer stone? Why was Amelia familiar with that name WHY did she feel a connection with this word?

She pushed it to the back of her mind. She was in awe. Then she looked back at Asillian.

"Don't worry if you do find me alluring. It's our pheromone that we give off. It only seems to have this effect on humans!"

Asillian had never felt this way about anybody but what he was feeling was admiration as he could tell this girl had her head screwed on plus she was unbelievably fiery in her own right.

"*Young one!*" shouted Jacobi, "concentrate."

"Yes. Sorry, Jacobi."

"Now," said Jacobi, looking at Ami (that's what her dad used to call her),"you've never heard of the freer stone?

Him.

He was the epitome of evil yet no one knew what *He* actually looked like but the voice of the evil one was so strong that if and when he spoke, would pop a human's head like a champagne cork!

"Why can I not get someone who knows what they're doing? It's like having my head stuck up my own arse!"

He was talking to his minions.

The Pit was a fiery hell hole. It was as hot as hell that hell could ever be. Every so often a plume of hell fire would shoot up and rise into the well that you could say was air?

Why every time do I ask you stupid cunts to do something do you go and do quite the opposite? If I had an ounce of power for every time this shit happened I would be able to smite the one they call God and cast him into Hell and take over the Earth and Heaven in a shitty heartbeat.

But no, not even you fucking inbred insubordinates could even do me that courtesy.

I'm surrounded by idiots!"

"But sire, it's like they knew we were coming ... they, they were prepared!" said one of the greeny red pustule-looking things.

"Then how do you suppose they did that? Cos blow me, I haven't got a fucking clue."

"We'll find out, sire. I'm sure of it," said a grotesque looking thing.

It looked like a huge overgrown marrow. At least that was what its belly amounted to.

On either side of its body was long octopus-looking tendrils and it could use its brain and telepathy to alter your state of mind quite drastically in the glimpse of a second.

The creature was called Apoch.

"Go with these imbeciles and find out the route of our problem. Okay?"

This was not a question, it was an order. So the minions scampered out of the chamber they were in and Apoch, unable able to walk, slithered out.

The elders
(Part 2)

There was uproar in the long hall where the 12 elders sat.

"How on earth has the seventh seal been broken unless that means that the unlawful one is brewing something in his pit of misery, deceit and lies?"

"We don't know this for sure," said one.

"But what if this sliver of information is right? Could the one they call *Him* be on the move?"

There was a huge droning noise but it could not be pinpointed.

"That sounds like the Karoth. (Bell of alarm!)"

"It is but what could this mean?" said one skittishly.

Ragnor!!

Suddenly there were blood curdling screams and sounds of metal striking metal.
   "I've come for you, elders," a deep booming voice bellowed.

"It can't be. We banished him millennia ago!"

All the elders stared at the double doors to the great hall in shock and horror.as they splintered into a thousand pieces.

As the dust settled a huge red figure made its way into the hall.

If you were to see it it you could call it a huge figure that could only be explained as the character of what people would consider the Devil.

It had wings at least four metres across and fangs that were to be honest terrifying ... easily, double the length of a full grown male baboon.

"Ragnor. No, it can't be. We banished you," stuttered one of the elders.

"Yes, but I am resurrected by *Him*, seeing how you elders forgot your sworn oaths to protect the seven seals! And now with the seventh seal broken you have unleashed all hell. *He* is coming and when he does he is going to come like a whirlwind, relentless and undying like the sun."

"You say this Ragnor but we have stopped you, and the one who shall not be named before. And we can do it again," screamed an elder who looked quite to be a fair older than the rest. He gripped his seat with frail fists.

Ha!

And to think I was going to keep you alive for last but No! I think I will kill you first seeing how your lord God has no power now the seventh seal is broken.

"You and your master will never get away with this you Vile Filth!" Another elder retorted.

"You say this but wasn't it you who relied on me when I was the protector God needed and not that old rival of mine Jacobi?

"Anyway enough of the chit-chat ... all your deaths await!"

With that Ragnor took out his bastard sword and began to slay each and every one of the helpless elders as blood laced the walls of the great hall.

And the elders were no more!

Ragnor Returns

"I have done your bidding, master."

"Ahhhhh!" came a very loud but kind of entrancing voice.

"I have one more task for you."

"Whatever it is master instruct away."

"The two angels Jacobi and his young apprentice Asillian are on a mission to get the freer stone and mend the seventh seal so it is right!"

"Yes? ... And what would you have me do, Sire?"

"I want you to hunt them down and slay the one they call Jacobi. Turn the little one against the order and poison his mind."

"That's easy. It's like child's play!"

"Then you shall not fail me, should you?"

"No, I shall not my lord. Consider Jacobi as good as dead."

With this the gigantic figure stepped out of the burning cesspit, and was gone.

Back with Amelia

Amelia had thought her meeting with the two angels had been quite peculiar. She had believed in a higher order ever since she was little but she never thought them true.

She needed to tell someone, she thought, but who?

The older angel had instructed her to go back to her home and think long and hard about where this freer stone may be?

She mused to herself while she climbed the stairs to her flat.

Boil

She got out her keys and went to open the flat of her door. Something wasn't right. She noticed the door was ajar and that when she entered there was no one there, but the flat had been turned upside down.

Clothes and drawers were thrown all about the place and it was the same in the kitchen with pots, pans and knives strewn about the lino floor.

She carefully walked towards the bedroom with a slight doubt and hesitation. Not knowing what was on the other side she slowly pushed the pine door open.

She looked around not finding anything or anyone. She heard a scratching noise like rats scurrying around. But she knew that was strange as the flat was usually well kept and Mrs Doyle would be on the council register if they knew the whole block was infested.

Then she heard a tiny voice speaking to itself. She strained to hear, but could just make it out ever so faintly.

"Master not going to be happy when he findssss out I haven't returned with anything!

Come on itsss got to be here somewhere. Where are you my golden looking temptress?"

Amelia peeked round the bed and saw a tiny looking creature. Maybe a puppy bulldog size and it had large green pustules all over its back.

She wasn't going to challenge or tackle the thing head on so she scanned round the room looking for something to catch the Damn thing in! She spotted a waste paper basket. Bingo, she thought.

She quietly came around the side of the bed being extra careful not to alert the beast.
    With that she took the bin and raised it over her head, bringing it down with a bang trapping the creature inside.

"Ha! Got you!" Amelia shouted.

"Huh, what? Oh, no let me out of here!"

The red creature screamed flashing its deadly fangs.

Amelia jumped back shocked and let go of the waste paper basket.

With this the tiny red creature scrabbled towards Amelia with ferocious pace. It lunged at her finger with the ring on, pulling her hand away just in time, Amelia screamed out in shock and horror. With that the creature fled out of the bedroom door only turning to say "We will rise again." It hissed and shot out of the door.

Amelia got her bearings and giggled crazily. What was this day coming to? She'd already found out that angels existed … and now a red imp demon creature and what only Amelia could describe as a chimera!

Amelia went to the bathroom to look at herself.

When she peered into the mirror she immediately thought about what the angels had said to her.

She brushed her hair back from her face and noticed her amber ring on her finger.

She heard a faint voice which sounded very familiar ...
   "The freer stone is right in front of you.
   All you have to do is look!"

"Did I just hear that or was it all in my head?"

She then looked at her hand for no particular reason. If that was my mum then how could she be talking to me from nowhere, its impossible! Well, she'd seen a pair of enormous angels this evening so why couldn't it be possible? And then she turned her attention to the rooms. How was she going to clean up all this mess?

Back at Annahiem the two angels Asillian and Jacobi walked towards the great hall. Asillian knew straightaway that there was something wrong.

"Approach with caution, master," he said "There's something amiss and I don't feel right."

Jacobi grunted in acknowledgement.

As they came to the huge oak doors they could see the doors were ajar and they had been broken by something monstrous.

"Stay back, Asillian while I investigate. If I should fall upon danger I will call you immediately."

"Yes, master," said Asillian.

As the much taller archangel came through the doors he immediately saw blood splashed across the walls, and then to his horror all the elders' heads pitted on spikes each above their own seats.

"Asillian!" called Jacobi.

"What? What is it, Master? What's the matter?" As the much younger angel came upon the decimated mess his heart dropped.

"What do we do, Master? They were our guidance and hierarchy"

"We must go and see an old friend about his skills and he owes me, as I think my old nemesis has something to do with this."

But how come The Lord saviour cant' do something about this?"

"He can't, Asillian. You of all people should know that as the seventh seal has been damaged and we as angels have to bring order to this whole mess."

"Certainly, master said Asillian thinking how God could help with a snap of his fingers or a wave of his hands!

Tull

The breeze was quite soothing as Tull ploughed his field ready for the next season of beetroot and potatoes.

The sun was nearly down but it was still warm on his naked top half. He was content in his own world in what you could call farmer life.

Tull was a huge brute of a man standing six foot six. His hands were like shovels, and his biceps were a quite impressive circumference ... 32 inches around. This was all due to his life as a farmer and all the heavy and back breaking work that he'd done with his father when he was still but a young teenager.

When he was nine he remembered his father saying to him.

"Tull, one day I will pass on, and the duties of the farm will fall to you. Do you think you will be able to handle the upkeep?"

Tull thought carefully about this and replied, "Yes, father!"

"Good, because I won't be around forever. You know that?"

Tull and his father never showed a lot of emotion to each other but they had an understanding that was solid.

Tull knew that his father loved him dearly, even if he was hard on him sometimes.

At the end of Tull's teenage years he discovered he could shape shift and this scared him.

His father had never mentioned anything like this to him but he knew somehow his father knew too.

He couldn't control it at first but when he put his mind to it he could become any living creature he desired!

All he would have to do was picture the thing he wanted to be and hey presto! he would suddenly become that thing!

Tull was an adventurous lad, he would sneak out at night and run and hunt as a wolf or a bear or for stealth he'd sometimes shape shift into a fox! Sprinting on all fours he would hunt with the pack or climb trees so far up when he was a bear to reach honeypots.

Tull lived where there were not many people around and it suited him. He was happy.

He had finished sowing the beetroot and potato seeds. With that he turned and as he did so he saw two figures rising over the huge grassy hill.

He didn't know the figure on the right but he definitely knew the one on the left.

As the pair drew closer he yelled out very loudly.

"Jacobi, is that you? I can't believe my eyes. By all the gods, is that you?"

"It is my old friend. How are you?"

Asillian looked to his master for some assurance. "Don't worry. He might look like a menacing figure of a man but he is the friendliest person I know. Just don't interrupt him and be polite."

"Whatever you say, master," said Asillian, still unsure.

An old debt

"Now I know you haven't come here just to see me, have you old friend?" said Tull giving Jacobi a very rough, manly pat on the back.

"I" see you've got a new accomplice," he said reaching across with his very broad arms.

Asillian reached out his palm to shake Tull's hand.

"Pleased to meet you night shifter," said Asillian knowing this is what Tull's shape-shifting alter ego was called.

"Well, tell me then Jacobi, why have you come here after all these years ... eh?"

"Well, remember that old debt?"

"Yes, you saved my life from the Cerebus."

"Well I need to call in that old debt."

"Well, of course. Ask away, my old friend."

"We need some supplies as well as a little favour of you, and to ask where the Holy manuscripts are kept as I think *He* has finally found a way of bringing chaos on both Heaven and Earth!"

"Crikey! Is it that bad? I need to get more acquainted with the world. Guess I've just become accustomed to this farmer's life," said Tull giving out a thunderous belly laugh.

"Come, come. You must be hungry. I have a cauldron of stew simmering inside."

"Asillian, stay out here. You can keep watch and have your rest later.

"Yes, sire," replied Asillian.

As Jacobi ducked under a huge centre beam that seemed to be holding the old house up, he glanced round the room and saw that Tull wasn't lying. Sure enough there on the fire was a huge cauldron of stew bubbling away.

Tull came across the room and picked up an old rag and a decent sized ladle to stir the stew.

"So tell me old friend, how is the young one getting along with you now that you have a new apprentice?"

"He's fine. Listens well, does as he's told and is quite skilled in the fighting arts.
   He has real potential!"

"And what about you? Do you believe in him? That's the most important thing because you know he will replace you when you decide to retire."

"Ha! Me, retire. Now I know you're joking … I'll keep fighting the good fight till someone takes my wings."

This was a saying of archangels because if their wings were removed they would become human, and would age as humans did.

"Well, my old friend would you do me a favour and pass me those bowls next to you?"

"Sure," said Jacobi.

Ragnor Rumours

"There's been talk round these parts that your old nemesis Ragnor is back and he's doing *his* work again!"

"Where have you heard this?" asked Jacobi with a hint of fear.

"Well, there's the trees. They whisper and also the wildlife are talking about it too. They say the seventh seal is broken and you and your companion Asillian are looking for the freer stone? And if this is true then I know why you're here."

"You do," Jacobi said surprisingly.

"Yes, yes you've come to me to see if I can make you a key to get into the gates, haven't you?"

"Well yes, I gathered that from all the turmoil that's going off in the forest. Trees are starting to die and no one, not even me, knows why."

"So do you still make the keys?" inquired Jacobi.

"Yes, and here," Tull said passing Jacobi a bowl full of stewed broth.

"I'm guessing you're going to need a few things from God's Armoury ... Yes?" he said taking in a big spoonful of stew.

"Only if it's not too much trouble, Tull?"

"Not at all. Now it's going to take me a few days to forge so you can happily sleep here and train on my sparring field with the young one ... if that's to your satisfaction?"

"Well, Indeed that would be wonderful!"

"Okay, now we've talked you can call in your apprentice. Asillian, isn't it?"

Jacobi ate the last bit of stew he had left and went outside to call in the younger angel.

As Asillian dreamed he tossed and turned in the hammock that Tull had kindly provided for him. Asillian didn't usually dream but on this occasion he did.

As he dreamed he could see death spawns everywhere. Demons and angels were all fighting against each other.
Then he heard a voice say "Wake up!"

He woke up with such a start that he nearly fell out of his hammock.
It was only Jacobi.
"You were mumbling in your sleep, are you okay, little one?"

"Yes, just a bad dream."

Asillian's test

"Remember, it isn't just skill when it comes to the arts, Asillian. It's sometimes about using your head and knowing when to use raw power!

"Right, I want you to strike that tree trunk as hard as you can."
"But why, sire? questioned Asillian.

"Because I said so and it's time you learnt what *He* can do in battle situations."

"Yes, master," said Asillian thinking how dumb this was as Jacobi had had him doing this for most of the morning.

45

"Draw your katana, instructed Jacobi.

Asillian reached behind his back to draw his katana. He pulled it out and it gave a very piercing ring as he did so. But a note to say hey, if you want your head chopping off you're in the right place.

Now strike!

As soon as Jacobi said this Asillian brought his stance to a high, one of the most destructive and aggressive stances there was.
   With a great arching motion Asillian brought his katana down on the stump with tremendous force.

Just as Asillian's katana was about to strike the stump it deflected and jolted all the way up his muscular but lithe arms and out of his palms!

He looked questionably at his mentor.

"See, it's not that easy is it?"

"Why did that happen, master? I don't understand!"

"Well, I put a protection spell over it. You can do it with any object. But it was a test to show you that even *He* will have the power to do this, as well as the most dangerous thing you must remember!

"Yes, what is it, master?"

"*He* is a deceiver and can make you see things that aren't there! That is his most greatest power and believe me he will use it if need be!

"Now listen! Tull is making us a key which will open the gates to another world but the only reason we need to go there is if Ragnor is back and we know the seventh seal has been damaged. We will need to acquire some tricks of our own. Do you understand?"

"Yes, master. But, sire what about the girl?"

We will come to her in due course. Her mother will protect her for the time being."

Tull was in his workshop, Asillian was astonished how he was working the metal to make the key. Sparks danced as he repeatedly arched his hammer over and over again hitting the lump of metal against the anvil which was slotted neatly and securely into a tree trunk.

"You move with ease, Tull," said Asillian.

"Well, I can shape shift … Asillian is it? What did you expect?"

Asillian laughed but not loudly as he didn't want to disrespect Tull's intelligence. "Can you really change into anything that is living with bones?"

"It is true, young apprentice. I will only show you once though as I'm not a performing seal. What animal would you like to see?" asked Tull.

Asillian thought deeply. "I'm not sure. Maybe an armadillo?" he spat out.

Tull giggled. "Why ever an armadillo may I ask?"

"I think they're intriguing but I think it would be harder for you to change into something smaller rather than larger … you understand Mr Tull?

"Truly, Asillian you're trying to challenge me I see. So an armadillo it is!"

The tall thick-set figure started to change ever so slowly, first Tull's head shrunk to a beigey, brown colour with a sticky-out snout.

Then his back started to move and shift. Suddenly with a *crack*! Tull's back miniaturised and became rounded with lots of armoured plates. And a small tail could be seen.

The armadillo gave a squeak of approval.

Asillian didn't really think about it but instinctively he picked Tull up and started to look into his tiny black eyes.

"Wow, that's amazing!"

With a shape-shifting clicking, Tull reshaped back to a man.

"Don't ever pick me up again, little one. I found that highly offensive what you just did."

"Oh, I'm sorry, Tull. I just got lost in the moment and was enthralled by the way you changed into such a tiny creature."

"Well, now you know that I can has that satisfied your curiosity?"

"Yes, indeed," said the young angel.

The curve

"Asillian," Jacobi shouted as Asillian spilt the rest of his breakfast down his tabard.

"Okay, I'm coming!" choked Asillian.

"Come, young one. We have much to go over."

They talked into what was to be around two hours before sunset. "So Jacobi, I mean master, where do you think Ragnor and *Him* will strike next?"

"Well, I think that depends where the girl is? I think we need some trinkets first though. We need to go to back to Garga's. If winds assist us we can get there in a day or so."

"I think Garga is hiding something."

"Back to his then first thing tomorrow, eh?"

"Yes, get some rest and we'll set off on the morrow."

"Yes, sire," he replied and headed over the rise and back towards Tull's.

Asillian thought about the one he'd felt feelings for over someone he'd first thought of. The feelings were bad but at first he felt the love, the warmth and the thought of the romance and the lust.

"Asillian, are you listening?" said Jacobi.
    "I can't concentrate, something is on my mind," retorted the young one.

"You think you can hit every target with just your mind."

"No, sire. I just thought ..."

"*Thought!* You couldn't think of anything with your mind so boggled!" Jacobi thought if ever this young one was going to learn it had to be through the *manner.

"If you know one thing it's concentrating on the true thing in life."

"And what is that, master?"

"Love, Asillian, Love can make magic move in the most mysterious way."

"How, master? As angels we don't feel attracted to the opposite sex."

"You must just believe. Move with your body."

"Okay, I will try, master"

As Asillian did this his bullet whipped by the tree that was in the way and found its mark hitting the target plum!

"But how?" questioned Asillian.

"You've got it now so never lose it. Okay?"

Yes, master I will not.

Back at Garga's

"Ssssooo, you are back? What is it I can do for you this time, Jacobi of Old?"

"We need protection from the Black Arts, something to protect us from these things, And you being a trader we hoped you would have something of this type Garga?

"Indeed."

Garga turned his back on the two archangels and looked behind him into rickety looking cupboards. Asillian looked at the demon creature and saw that Garga didn't just have horns on his head but miniature horns all the way up his backbone. You could hardly notice this though as he had an old potato sack draped across his body.

"Ah, ha! Here we have the shield of Titan. It is made of the hardest substance known to man, god and demon."

The shield gleamed as Garga held it up with great difficulty.

"Now, Old one," he spoke to Jacobi "if you hold it you will the shield go into defensive mode so just sit back and see what happens."

Jacobi took the shield with ease from Garga. it weighed nothing to the old archangel.
    Stand back young one! He said as he raised the shield and willed it like Garga had instructed.

With an enormous chinging sound the shield came all the way around the huge angel and protected everything even with his huge expanse the shield created like a chrome ball around the huge angel.

"Whoa!" exclaimed Asillian.

Then as the angel with the shield willed it to its normal size again, it obeyed and was a shield again.

"Now for the Asillian, first of his name. Something with oomph,! I think."

With that Garga whipped round and rooted through the cupboard throwing objects about the place.

Ahhhh ... here!

Garga turned around and produced silver gloves ... chain mail gloves

"Try these, Asillian."

Asillian looked for confirmation from the older and wiser angel.

Jacobi nodded.

He slipped them on. "What do they actually do apart from protect me from demon bites and scrapes?"

Garga explained that he would have to go outside if they both wanted to see the gloves work.

"Now thesssee are the greaves and gloves of power!"

"Try smashing that rock," said Garga with delight.

"Are you mad? I'll break my hand!"

"Not with those on you won't. Just try."

So Asillian moved over to the rock and hit out at it.

The rock split straight down the middle with great ease, Asillian was surprised as the rock was a rock!

"Sssoooo, Asillian … Jacobi is there anything else I can help you with?"

"I think that will be all, Garga," said Jacobi.

"Come Asillian, we need to get back to Tull."

"Ahhhh … Tull. How is the shape-shifting fiend?"
    Garga called him a fiend, as he was jealous that he could not do what the shape shifter could do.

"He's fine, Garga!"

"Right, well tell him that old Garga was asking about him, won't you?"

"Not sure he'll like it, but I will, Garga."

"Well, we must leave now so keep out of trouble Garga! If we find out you're back to your old ways we will return!"

"Okay, okay, I understand. Safe journey to you, Jacobi."
    "And you also Asillian, first of his name ...

"Yes, Garga and thank you!"

The Vow

As Asillian and Jacobi left Garga's Jacobi turned to Asillian and said, "Asillian never ever say thank you to a demon even if he is neutral. Do you understand?"

"Yes, master but why not?

"Because if you say that the demon being a demon regardless if he is neutral or not will automatically think that you are in his debt! And being in debt with a demon is a situation you do not want to get yourself into. Okay, is that clear?"

"Yes, Jacobi I will remember that, master."

"Always?" asked the bigger archangel.

"Always!" replied Asillian feeling like a scorned child.

The Key

As Tull worked on what was becoming the key, he turned to the younger angel and asked him what he thought of all this palaver.

Asillian just shrugged and to Tull it showed that he wasn't bothered. He had other things on his mind like how was he meant to temper his feelings for this human he thought about constantly.

He thought about the curve and how love affected the bullet's trajectory.

Then he suddenly gave a thought to Tull as he knew he was a shape shifter but he was still human in a way.

"Tull, may I ask you a question?"

"Ask away, Asillian," he said.

"Have you ever been in love?"

With this Tull stopped hammering the piece of steel that was soon to be the finished piece of the key.

"Asillian, why do you ask that?"

"Well ... it's just ..." he trailed off.

"Out with it!" demanded Tull. "You can't start a question then not finish what you were going to say ... so what is it? What's bothering you?"

"You'll promise not to tell Jacobi, won't you?"

"Okay, Asillian. I promise," said the great stature of a man.

"Well, I think I'm in love with the young girl who we've been protecting."

"I thought angels couldn't fall in love because of the heavenly and mighty love they have for their maker … Lord God?"

"We can love but I just can't figure it out. It's strange."

"Anyway, I'm over that now. Have you nearly finished the key? He questioned.

"Go and have some broth. You look hungry I promise by the time you've finished it, I will have finished the key," he said very assuredly.

Rowan and Amelia

As Amelia left her apartment she wondered how much trouble she was actually in. She looked down and saw she was rubbing her ring unconsciously.

She was afraid as well as worried so she went to seek guidance from the only other person she knew would believe her, her college teacher Rowan.

As the college bell rang to signal the end of the day, Rowan packed his journals and books that were all studies about really old school religion, then raised his voice over the alarm bell that was ringing.

"Don't forget next month's exam. I hope you all study hard and come up with some excellent work, Bye guys."

Rowan was averagely tall, thin and had hair like Colin Farrell in *Alexander*, except that his was a mouse brown, and comical round rimmed spectacles.

There was a fierce wrapping on the classroom door!

"Enter," he said.

With this Amelia came rushing through the door panicking and flustered.

"*You've* got to help me, Rowan. I don't know what else to do."

"Slow down!" he said reassuringly as he could see that she was in a really bad state.

"Take a breath and tell me the problem."

"You're not going to believe me and I don't know how to say this."

"Calm down, Amelia! I'm sure if you stop panicking everything will be okay."

"Well, Rowan when I was on the metro the other day I could feel a sort of presence watching me. I got off the metro and continued on my way. Suddenly as I came into an alleyway a chimera set about me."

"Whhaat! Surely your mistaken chimeras are folklore and not real, Amelia. You know that, don't you?"

"I know but I couldn't believe it myself. Then after about 10 seconds of me seeing this creature there was a flash of light and two winged humans killed it I think they were angels!"

Rowan looked at her in disbelief but from how distraught and all the panic he could see in her face, he knew she wasn't joking.

"Hold your horses, Amelia! You're saying you saw a mythological creature and two others who appeared to be angels?"

"Yes, that exactly right. Y-O-U do believe me, don't you? After all you've got a major in all of this stuff. Right?"

"Yes, but no-one's heard of these things you speak about since the Crusades. And even before the birth of Christ! Holy shit, this is extraordinary."

After what seemed to be a lifetime, Amelia had gone through all the day's events from the archangels to the chimera and the little red imp creature that she'd caught in the waste bin, but which later escaped.

Amelia found herself rubbing the amber stoned ring that her mother had passed down to her.

"Every time I think about what the angels said to me I find myself turning this ring around or checking if it's still there."

"Oh my god, that's it, the freer stone," screamed Rowan at the top of his voice. "That's what they've been searching for and just think, it's the ring your mother wanted you to have for a special reason. What else could it be if not the freer stone? Right?"

"Yes, I wondered why that evil little creature ransacked my flat. His master must have told him whereabouts it was located. But I suppose it's a mighty good job he didn't, eh?

The barren lands

Asillian looked stressed to Jacobi. So Jacobi asked him if he was okay.

"You okay, young one?"

"Yes, master. Just confused."

"Why, what's the matter?"

"Well, I've been thinking about what you said about the curve and how I can alter the trajectory of my bullets with just the thought of love."

"Yes and what do you think about that?"

"Well, Jacobi. I've been thinking about it and I'm really confused."

"Well, tell me while we fly."

"Yes, wise one", Asillian said.
    With that Jacobi jumped a metre into the air and gave a mighty beat of his wings rising easily into the sky.

Asillian did exactly the same, and was not far behind his teacher.

"So, Asillian tell me what's confusing you?"

"Well, it's that you taught me about the curve and love. Right?"

"Go on!" his master willed.

"Yes, but you told me to think of love and now whenever I think about love I immediately start to think about the girl we saved from the chimera and it's weighing on me heavily master."

"Well young one, it seems to me your heart is ruling your head and you have a case of what they call the blues!"

"The blues?" questioned Asillian.

"Yes, it's when you have a thought about someone or something. And if I'm right you're in love with this girl, which is causing feelings that you've never felt before!"

"But I thought angels can't love humans and can only have love for their creator and the one who rules us in heaven? God!"

"That is true Asillian but you have to be aware what your feelings for her you will have to shun."

"Okay, master I will try and I will put it to the back of my mind."

"And make sure it stays there," commanded Jacobi in his hoarse voice. "Now come, take the lead. I will give you a head start but let's still see if you're quick enough to keep up with me."

"Okay, Jacobi but I'm warning you I've got a little quicker."

With that Jacobi gave an enormous beat of his wings and left Asillian in an instance.

Right that's it, Asillian thought. Suddenly, he hit turbo speed as he caught up to Jacobi. He smirked and beat his wings again and again, touching the sound of speed as he raced through the sky like a Concorde.

"Come on loser," he shouted back at Jacobi. "What's the matter? Too quick for ya!"

Then in an instance Jacobi was about to follow when out of nowhere came Ragnor. "Ha!" he shrieked as he batted Asillian out of the sky.

"Guess who's back?"

Jacobi was not scared; he was only concerned with where Asillian had disappeared to.

"How are you my old nemesis? Feeling old? You look it. And wow the Lord still hasn't given you back the eye I stole off you. Well I suppose that's too damn rotten. How about you tell me where the girl is and I promise to leave her in one piece? How does that tickle your fancy? You betrayed me once. I won't make a second mistake."

"Ohhhhh, I'm frightened, very frightened. I'm shaking out of my taut red skin."

"You will be, bastard!"

The Hell Pit

He watched as Boil advanced hopping between the red hot scorching stalagmites, and lava pits.

"Where have you been, you insolent shit?" he boomed

"Massster I went to the place where the girl lived but I am afraid your Excccellence, the stone wasn't there."

"What?"

"But master, I cannot go again. I was nearly trapped."

"Hovelshit! You will do as I bid and don't forget if you succeed I will reward you handsomely How does that sound, Boil?"

"Yes, Massster," Boil said as he quickly flicked his green, gaseous tongue in and out.

"Now go find the stone. Ragnor is dealing with the so called watchers."

"It is your will, sssire." With that Boil scurried off to go and find the thing that would help decide whether Hell would overcome Heaven and Earth.

60

Rowan's investigation

"Quickly, let's go to the college library, I'm sure we can find a lot more out there."

"Sure," Amelia replied, as she took in that Rowan wasn't even blinking an eyelid to the story she had just told him.

The fight above the barren lands

"So you think you can just bounce my accomplice and even think that *He* can overrun Hell, Heaven and Earth?"

"Why not? After all it was you who drove me to it, wasn't it master?"

"Never say that word to me again, Ragnor. You chose your own path."

"Okay … master!" Ragnor growled.

With that there was a shout from Asillian. "Master? What does he mean by master?" he said.

"Never mind that now, young one. Just concentrate as this demon filth has a lot of deceptive tactics lined up for us."

"I certainly have, and your young apprentice is going to be the first to learn how powerful I have become."
    Swiftly, Ragnor started to look like he was feinting to go left after Asillian but strafed left, claws out gleaming ready to hack out Jacobi's last good eye.

"Not so fast, scum," said Jacobi as he reached around for his staff of righteousness.

Asillian closed his eyes and prayed.

Suddenly there was a bone crunching thud.

Asillian opened his eyes and saw that his partner, had blocked the giant demon's claw, with only a half a second to spare.

Within an instance Asillian was trading blow for blow with Ragnor while Jacobi was recovering from the impact from the vile demon.

"So you think you can take the other eye of my master? Well, we can all dream."

"Ah ... You fool. Don't you see he was once my master at one point?"

"W-what?" said a shocked Asillian.

"Aawww ... He hasn't told you yet? Never mind, he will. Well I'm afraid if the girl isn't with you I must depart."
    And with that Ragnor dissipated into thin air!

"We will resume this, Asillian. Don't you fret young one. He will pay!"

"He certainly will, master ... but what did he mean when he called you master?"

"That doesn't matter right now Asillian. Just focus like you've never focused before."

The college archives

As Rowan sifted through the copious amount of books that were at his disposal, he couldn't help thinking how shocking and daunting it was to find out that there were demons below and they wanted to come and destroy Earth!

"Ah, here it is, the angels, God and the seventh seal!"

Amelia looked bewildered and just stared blankly at Rowan.

He checked the index and saw the underlying text which said the seventh seal.

"Right, here is the seventh seal. According to this there are seven seals that protect Earth from Hell. There are three more but the main one is the seventh seal. And that says, that is the one which God watches over.

"If the seventh seal is damaged for too long then demons of all kinds can be free to roam the Earth!"
   "Jesus!" gasped Amelia putting her hand to her mouth.

"So this could be the end after all! But why am I involved?"

Rowan read further down the page and answered.
   "It describes here a chosen one that has a special stone. That will bring about the fall of Hell if she can defeat *Him*."
   "Who is *Him*?" she asked.

"The Devil of course," replied Rowan.

"Holy mother ... that means I'm in danger. Right?" There's more. If *He* gets hold of the stone then the power will switch in *His* favour!

Rowan looked at her and could see she was about to break down into tears.

"Don't worry. You said there were angels. Right?"

"Yes", she said toughening up immediately. "We're gonna need their help."

"So where shall we go?"

"Well, the younger looking angel told me that all I have to do is think about them and they will appear."

"Well, what are you waiting for? Do it and do it quickly, for I feel we are in grave danger Amelia.

Bane

The cavern hissed with the violent heat that was all around.

"Where is *He*? That fool should have been here by now with news of his victory."

Just as *He* said this there was a blur of purple gas and Ragnor appeared.

"Well?"

The huge winged figure bent down on one knee and bowed his head.

"Master ...

"Yes."

"I failed to kill the old one."

"What?" He boomed shaking the stalagmites and the whole underground cesspit.

"Well, I dealt with the youngest, he was no match for me. But my old master thwarted me, he had some sort of staff that stopped my talons dead."

"So you're thinking that you need a little help ... is that it?"

"I don't mean to anger you but yes some help would be greatly appreciated, sire."

"Here ..."

Ragnor raised his hideous horned skull and saw an amazing weapon. He couldn't see all of it as it rose out of a pool of lava.

"This ... is Bane ... my greatest creation."

Ragnor could see the whole weapon now. He could see a blade of such reckoning and so bulky that he was sure he could never be able to wield it, even though he had gigantic muscles.

"Whenever this weapon moves it absorbs the souls of its victims, doubling and then quadrupling the wielder's strength.

"You must not fail me this time, Ragnor. Do you understand?
     "Yes, sire. I understand."

"So, what are you waiting for? Take Bane and go."
     "But master, this blade is enormous. How will I ever be able to wield it?"

"Take it and see, you fool!"

With that Ragnor took Bane in his talon-filled grasp lifting it easily out of the lava pool. Immediately Ragnor felt a gigantic rush of power flow through his whole body. Wow … He shadowed a few blows on an imaginary foe. He found it very manoeuvrable and light.

"You see! The souls that are already in it make Bane as light as any other weapon. Make it a part of you and you shall bring down any enemy you desire. , Do you understand?"

"Truly, you are great, master," Ragnor said in awe. "I will do as you bid. Shall I go after the girl or the two thorns in your side?

"No! You shall go and tell them all that I am gaining strength all the time and I shall soon lead all my followers to victory!"

"As you bid, sire."
And with that Ragnor turned and flew out of the huge cavern.

The switch

"Amelia what are you thinking about? You look a million miles away."

"Oh nothing, I was just thinking if that small creature comes back looking for my ring we need to swap it with something so if he does obtain it, then it will be worthless."

"Whoa … that's a terrific idea but what can we switch it with?"

Think, Amelia. Think, she thought to herself.
"Aha! Got it. We could go to an arts and crafts shop and find something there that resembles my mother's ring and swap

them. Then hide the ring in a place where no-one will ever find it. What do you think?"

"That's sound good to me. Let's go to my car and then we can drive into town."

As Rowan drove Amelia into the middle of town the streets looked empty.

"Where shall I park?" said Rowan.

"Just here will do," replied Amelia.

Amelia could see Celeste's weird and wonderful shop right on the corner of Cranshaw and Minister.

"I won't be long," said Amelia.

"Okay, but be quick. It doesn't look very promising around here," replied Rowan.

Amelia opened the passenger seat door and stepped out into the street. She looked both ways then quickly entered the shop.

There was a "chime" and she entered.

Once Amelia was inside it was very misleading as the shop looked tiny from the outside but was very deceptive as the interior was quite spacious. At one end there were dream catches and burning incense. This reminded Amelia of the incense that her mother would get her father to burn in the living room. This immediately made her feel very relaxed.

"Hello," chirped Amelia.

"Can I help you?" came a voice from the back of the shop.

"Yes, I'm just looking."

As Amelia scanned the ridiculous amount of items and oddities that were scattered around the shop, her eyes focused on a basket full of rings that were marked in full block capital letters with the price tag of £3.50.

One of the mood rings looked exactly like the one she was wearing.

"Could I please have one of these?" Amelia asked in a very relaxed sort of way.

"Oh! Very good choice. Do you know what size you are?" asked the woman who came into view now.

No more than 55, she walked over to where Amelia was standing. Amelia noticed that she had deep aquamarine eyes and she could feel her presence very much. Amelia sensed she was very warm-hearted and had a nurturing side to her. She wasn't sure why or how she could tell this but she felt very much at ease with her.

The woman had greyish white hair and looked well for her age.

"Could I have that the amber coloured one please?" Amelia said reaching inside her jeans for a £5 note. "And I think I'm a 'P'."

"Very good and would you like a blessing or does anything else catch your eye?"

"Well," said Amelia not wanting to seem ungrateful, "how much extra is the reading?"

"Well, seeing how you purchased something I will give you one for free," said the woman.

"Oh, okay," replied Amelia surprised.

"I will need to see your palm," said the woman.

"Right, let me have a gander," said the woman putting on her spectacles that she fixed on a lanyard around her neck.

"Well, Amelia It seems you are headstrong and you get that from your father. I can also see you have untapped potential which comes from your mother's side. Oh, and what's this? You've had a very strange few days. It seems you've met some very interesting people. You could say they're your guardian angels.

"And I see you have a quest or journey that you are about to embark on.

"Now, Amelia listen when I say this journey or quest you are about to go on is going to test your faith but do not dismay. I can see that you have nothing but love in your heart and this will see you through any obstacles that may come across your path."

"Really! How do you know all this?"

"Let's just say it's intuition and a little bit of fate and destiny!"

Amelia looked at her watch and realised she'd been with the woman for at least half an hour!

"I am sorry," she said, "but I have to go. I have a friend waiting for me outside. You understand, don't you?"

"Of course, but just remember with love comes loss. Now here you go," the woman said passing Amelia her gift-wrapped mood ring. "And go in peace", said the woman.

"Right. Okay, thank you ever so much, Celeste. Have a great day!"

"Oh, all the better that I met you Amelia. Now go to your friend who might think you've got lost," chuckled Celeste.

With that Amelia rushed for the door and was gone.

"What took you so long? I said be quick."

"I know but there was this really interesting woman named Celeste and ..."

"Never mind that now, just get in. We need to go," ordered Rowan. "Did you get what you were looking for?"

"Yep," replied Amelia showing him the gift-wrapped ring.
    "I'm going to put the real one into the glove box and wear the fake one as a guise."

"Okay, well if you're sure?"

"I am," replied Amelia, "besides no one's going to be looking in the windows of this death trap," she said jokingly.

"Well, aww geez, thanks a bunch."

With that Amelia took off the ring her mum had given to her and swapped it for the mood ring.

"Wow, that does look the same. So where to now?" said Rowan.

Tull's promise

"Well here it is. My hard work and energy has gone into this. I hope you feel my debt to you is paid now Jacobi?"

"Well, yes most certainly, Tull."

"With this we can go to the door past the great hall."

"What will we find there master Jacobi?" asked the younger angel.

"Well, the tabards suggest if ever God was waylaid with something then we should go through the doors at the back of the great hall.

"And this is where we'll find answers?" said Asillian.

"Positive," replied his mentor.

Just as Asillian and Jacobi turned to leave Tull piped up. "If you see that devious meddler Ragnor tell him to come and settle his score with me."

"Will do my old friend and thanks again," said Jacobi.

"Come young one we must go to the great hall! This key that Tull made should see us right."

As Asillian and Jacobi entered the great hall there were lesser angels their cleaning up the mess that Ragnor had wreaked: Gore off the walls and heads on spikes.

As they came to the back of the hall Asillian could see that there was no door. In fact it was just a plain wall of marble.

"I don't understand, master? Where's the door?"

"Patience, Asillian."

Jacobi held out the key to the wall ... and the wall started to shift and manoeuvre in a way where there was a slight shadow that looked to Asillian like a keyhole!

"There, master," he said, astonished.

"Yes, I see it," confirmed Jacobi.

Jacobi pushed the key that his old friend had forged for them and within an instance the wall became a door.

"What now?" said Asillian.

"Give it a push," requested Jacobi.

So Asillian pushed the wall ever so slightly and the door opened.

"Now whatever you see beyond here you must never tell a soul. Do you understand?" asked Jacobi.

"Okay, I won't," he said.

"The only reason I say this is because if God knew you were here I'd be in a lot of trouble as only grandmaster angels are allowed beyond this point."

So Jacobi led the way. It was dark so Jacobi instructed Asillian to take one of the torches off the wall, and light it with his elemental powers.

Asillian did this with so much ease that Jacobi congratulated him.

"I learn from the best master," said Asillian.

There were cobwebs everywhere and the ceiling was very low so Jacobi and Asillian had to stoop so they wouldn't catch their heads or wings.
They walked for what seemed like an age.
Eventually they came to a massive room that was coloured a brilliant sheen of white. The room seemed to emanate its own light so Asillian killed the flame that was burning on the torch. As they came further in Asillian could see scrolls upon scrolls of parchment resting on great oak shelves.

"This is the scriptures room, Asillian where fate and history all have their place."

"Wow!" exclaimed Asillian, his jaw hanging open. "Whoever knew all this was here? It's astonishing!"

"Let me see. Now here we are," said Jacobi pulling out a scroll of parchment.

He unrolled it and began to read:

"If this day should come when I am not instructing angels or watching over mankind I want you to know there is always faith for him who has faith in me, and they will be everlasting. So I say, Lord Almighty.

"He has tried many times to rule Heaven, Earth and Hell but there is one thing that He will not be able to do and that is influence the mind of the chosen one ... they shall be the protector of the Freer's Stone and will bring balance back to Heaven, Earth and all mankind.

"With this said if you are reading this then you must not let the chosen one out of your sight.
    And protect them at all costs.
    So I proclaim."

"So you know what this means," Jacobi said to Asillian.

"Yes, we need to find the girl! What are we waiting for? Let's go!"

With that the angels turned back and headed off at a low but deftly sprint.

Boil's second attempt
Chapter 1

As Rowan's car sped away Boil looked on in anger.

"Well, I'd better go and see what she went in there for?

The bell on Celeste's shop jingled as Boil crept in.

"Hello?" said Celeste … "Hello, who's there?"

Celeste looked around the shop scanning everywhere. She could sense danger as she was a medium.
   "Whoever you are come out Immediately!"

Boil laughed a little skittishly but it was enough to scare Celeste.
   "Tell me what the girl wanted," said Boil, devilishly.

"Not before you tell me who you are and what you want?" retorted Celeste bravely.

"I won't tell you nothing, *Witch!*"
   With that Boil came into view.

Celeste nearly burst into laughter, but restrained herself as she did not know how dangerous this little imp was.

"Now *Witch* tell me what the girl came here for," said Boil shooting across the floor at an alarming speed.

"Oh, my goodness," cried Celeste as Boil scaled her leg knocking her to the floor.

Celeste was dazed by the fall. When her head had stopped swimming she opened her eyes, and saw that the bright red imp creature had climbed up on her chest making it hard for her to breathe.

"Tell me, Peagan, what did the girl want?" he hissed as his tongue flicked in and out all the while.

Celeste thought about being brave but the demon looked dangerous.

"Okay, she wanted a mood ring ... j..j..just a mood ring. That's all. Now leave me be creature," Celeste said panicking.

"I'm afraid I can leave no witnesses," said Boil sinking his venomous fangs into her throat. The poison would only make her forget the whole experience and not kill her luckily.

Then he skittered out the shop with a devious giggle.

Chapter 2

Boil went to the side of an alley and looked into a dustbin lid. He hawked up some venom and spat it into the lid. Within an instant there were billows of nauseous, green gas. A murky image came into view.

Then there was a voice; it was *Him*!

"Hello, S-s-sire. It's me, Boil. The girl stopped off at a witch's domain. I didn't follow her in because of the spells she might have had ... you understand?

But I did find out that she bought a mood ring for some reason?"

"That's it," he laughed. "The ring ... That's the opening that we need ... Don't you see, Boil, the stone is the ring!"

"Ah, now I sseee, ssire. Do you want me to take action?"

"Yes ... that would be most acceptable. But go now. I see her going to the graveyard in the near future but be wary, I have undead on alert," he said.

Sure enough the gas dissipated and the murky image was gone.

The graveyard it is then, Boil said to himself.

"Mum?"

As Amelia was travelling with Rowan in the little red Metro, she felt that there was a presence in the car with them. She wasn't bothered though as the presence felt calming and friendly.

Amelia always remembered her mother had told her father that she was gifted and she had a sixth sense, when it came to faith and religion.

"You feel that?" she said to Rowan.
   Rowan stared blankly at her.

The presence was telling her to go to the graveyard, willing her to visit her father's grave.

Rowan could see something was occupying Amelia's mind so he asked her what she was thinking. She said they needed to visit her father's tombstone!

"Okay if that's what you really feel you want to do," Rowan said without argument. He turned the Metro around and headed for Peel Hill.

"Can you sense her, master?" asked Asillian.

"Yes," said Jacobi, "she seems to be heading for the graveyard which could be dangerous seeing how the seventh seal is damaged and *He* can see most things now.

"So keep your wits about you and we will do what we can. But come now we must hurry."

"Why the graveyard?" said Rowan.

"Just stop talking and drive," said Amelia very abruptly as she was annoyed and couldn't understand what was the source.

"So what are these angels like? Do they look how the legends tell them?"

Amelia thought this was a fair question so she answered. "Yes, they're magnificent ... but hell are they tall!"
  Once Amelia started thinking about the angels she could hear the older angel's soothing, masculine voice.

"Me and Asillian will meet you at the place where your father rests."

Knowing this, Amelia immediately felt a lot calmer and safer within herself.
  The journey took them about 25 minutes out of town and was on the verge of Peel Hill, which was set next to the church and the graveyard, where all the moss-covered tombstones could be seen.
  As Amelia got out of the little red Metro it had started to rain but not drizzle. It was a downpour.

"Great ... that's all we need!"

Rowan got out of the car and came round to give Amelia her coat and put on his waterproof jacket as well.

"Are we good?" He said.

"Yeah, let's go," replied Amelia shivering.

Ragnor spied and saw the two figures come into view walking in between the graves.
  "Like lambs to the slaughter," he scoffed.

He called for Bane and the weapon appeared out of thin air into his deadly talons. The blade whispered with what was the echo of a thousand dead souls.

"Don't worry, Bane," he said to the weapon that he had been given," you shall soon have two more souls to feed on!"

Ragnor had been given a spell by *Him*. It was a dead will rise spell. As Ragnor worked the magic on two graves, Amelia turned with Rowan and knelt at her father's gravestone.

The odd couple

"What do you mean I never looked after you when we were alive?" said Morti. His flesh crawled with rancid maggots.

"Well," said Rita, "you never put the washing out when I asked you to plus you never ever ran me a bath with candles."

"Oh shut up, woman," he mumbled. As he did so his jaw fell off.

"See, I even have to look after you now we're both dead!"

"Cut it out you two. Now listen, if you want to get some peace and rest then I should take those two humans alive ... and be quick about it!"

"Yeah, yeah Ragnor apprentice of *Him* ... give us a break. We're over 250 years old for Pete's sake ... Our bones ache, mister!"

"Just do as you are bid," said the huge beast.

"Well, how do we go about this, dearest? Shall we sneak attack them or wear disguises?"

"Disguises," said Ragnor waving his razor sharp talon over the two corpses.

Instantly they took on skin and flesh and were whole again.

"Hurry as this illusion spell only lasts a few minutes."

"Right you are," chirped Morti. "Come on, dearie."

The dead rise

"Hello there! How are you?"

"We're here to visit our dead son's grave from the war. His name's Larry." Rita wept fake tears into her yellowed hanky.

"Yes, yes, our son was a fighter in the 32nd battalion you know," interrupted Morti pretending to comfort his wife.

"Oh, I'm sorry. I forgot to introduce myself. My name's Rita and this is my husband Morti." "Pleased to meet you," said Rita holding out her liver-spotted hand.

Amelia was a little revolted because of the odour coming from the couple.

"Yes, nice to meet you," she said disgusted. "We're here to visit Clive, my father's grave.

"Oh bless! What did he die from?" said a nosey Rita.

"Cancer," replied Amelia. She could feel herself welling up inside as she fought back tears.

"Aww!! Shame," said Morti.

As Ragnor stared on impatiently wondering what the two dead fogies were on about he could see the spell would soon be wearing off.

"Hurry you dimwits!" he mumbled.

Amelia kissed her hand and touched the top of her father's gravestone. "Miss you, dad," she said so only she heard.

"And who is this fine gentleman? Your older brother perhaps?"

"No, he's my old college teacher Rowan."

"Rowan, grand to meet you," said Morti stretching out his also liver-spotted hand.

Rowan shook Morti's hand which to Amelia's horror broke off at the wrist!

"Run!" screamed Rowan.

Out of nowhere

Amelia nearly twisted her ankle running from the two decaying corpses.

"Hurry, Rowan," shouted Amelia.

"What are they?" said Rowan fearfully.

"The undead," cried Asillian swooping in with a beat of his wings.

Rowan looked on in awe as the two angels landed in the graveyard just metres from where they were.

"You ready, little one?" said Jacobi assertively.

"Ready as ever," came the reply.

"See what you can do with those gauntlets of yours," Jacobi said.

"Sure," said Asillian.

In an instance Jacobi had noticed Ragnor emerging from a host of grave stones nearby ... well, it was hard to miss the great hulking red demon. And his blazing weapon.

"Go now, Asillian!" ordered Jacobi. "Ill take care of my old emissary," he assured.

"Okay," cried Asillian.

"But make sure you are careful, old one"

"There's still fight in this old dog yet," replied Jacobi. "Go, I'll be fine."
    Rita and Morti looked at each other and jointly said, "Oh, shit!"

The two corpses disintegrated into skeletal ash.

"You'll never get the freer stone," screamed Amelia.
    "And if you do you'll have to get through me first," Rowan said convincingly.

"Bah! You humans are no match for me. I could easily crush you with a click of my fingers."

"I'm not going to let that happen now, am I Ragnor?"

"Well you can try and stop me if you wish but I assure you won't, also you remember this blade, do you not?"

Asillian looked over to his teacher with a certain look on his face. It was a look that said whatever else have you not told me?

"Oh, he doesn't know. Why don't you enlighten him, Jacobi?"

"He thinks that because when I was his teacher and mentor that if he beat me in a hand to hand duel I would retire as an archangel and let him take over and teach. He became desperate when he couldn't better me and snatched out my eye with his fingers and nails.

From that moment on the order banished him to live the rest of his miserable life in Hell.

"So," Interrupted Ragnor, "I used to be an archangel. But just look at me now!" He cackled.

Ragnor had had enough of his time wasting. Now he would feel the full force of Bane!

Ragnor made a fist and mumbled some incantation then whoosh! the flame became alight.

"Great, who do I fight?" said Asillian.

"Keep Amelia and Rowan safe. I just need a few minutes with this cretin."

Rowan was in awe of the two vastly taller angels, and man, was their wing span enormous.

It was at times like these that Rowan wished he had his Polaroid camera with him. The college professors would scoff if he showed them real concrete evidence of the afterlife.

He was now worried as he knew they were after the keeper stone.

"Where is it?" exclaimed Rowan.

"The woman at the shop said the ring had special powers, and that I could use them of my own free will if need be," said Amelia.

"And when did she say use it, because we are running short on time here? If you haven't noticed she said when all other options are depleted I should use it then."

The Dead Rise

Boil had made it to the graveyard just in time. He began hopping and skipping between the tombstones, spitting acrid, green acid onto the roses and wreaths of withered flowers. Almost instantly hands and skulls began to rise out of the ground. Asillian instructed the two of them to flee into the church, as no evil could reach them there. "You got this little one." "Yes, you concentrate on that traitor of an understudy."

... And so it begins, thought the two archangels telepathically.

Ragnor's Day

Ragnor was not always beastly looking. He was, in fact, one of the more divine, well-mannered looking angels. He was a good size and always ate fruit and plenty of bread. Angels didn't eat meat ...

"Where's Ragnor?" exclaimed Jacobi. "Over by the sparring grounds," replied the angel who would run/fly around doing errands for Jacobi. "Thank you, dismissed," ordered Jacobi. With that the angel appeared to glide away on his feet. Jacobi noticed he hadn't fully developed his wings yet. "Nice sneakers, Sketch"

Jacobi said. "Thanks," said Sketch, and with that the young angel was gone from sight.

"Ha, ha, ha. You do know it's your downward strokes that lead
you astray and give away your next move, don't you, Ragnor?"
"Well, I have been practising, master, I think I deserve a chance of
being a fully-fledged angel, don't you?" "Oh, so you think you're
big enough to take on old Jacobi here?" "I ... I ... I was just saying,
master." "Now, come on ... rest your weapon and come full circle". "You sure?" Ragnor said, surprised. "We begin at the point
of the shadow, if that's okay with you?", "or we could wait till
the crack of dawn". "Do I hear you correctly, master? If I make
you yield, I can become a fully-fledged angel?". "Yes, those are
the rules and my terms Ragnor."

This was no ordinary throw down; it was a challenge.

The rules were that two angels entered and when the other angel yielded the other angel won. And that would be that!

They could both hear metal resounding off metal. They shocked
the angel who was practising on his lonesome upon a half sawn
log.

"You know how this works, Squirt. Whoever yields first los-
es, okay?"

"Yes, sir," said the much smaller graduate angel.

Both the angels had gathered quite a crowd now.as Jacobi
dropped his staff and the other trinkets attached to his belt.

Ragnor having been newly trained only had a falchion which
he dropped.

They eyed each other up then entered the sand circle with
such attentive concentration towards each other.

Jacobi feinted right while leaning to the left punching Ragnor
square on the cheek. A bruise became apparent immediately.

"Yield?" Jacobi asked.

"Never!" screamed Ragnor.

Ragnor timed his sprint to perfection spearing Jacobi right in the middle of his mid-section, which took Jacobi to the ground.
    The old angel was surprised.

"Do you yield?" Ragnor said while struggling to get a choke hold round the much bigger angel's head.
    "Do you Ragnor?" asked Jacobi.
    "I am in the bargaining seat here!"
    "Well if that is the case make me yield!"

"There's only one way I will ever say those words and that is when I think you are ready," instructed Jacobi.

Ragnor still had the choke hold on Jacobi, who was never going to concede. Ragnor could see it in his eyes.
    "So just take it as a lesson learnt and be on your way Ragnor."
He calmed himself.
    "Okay, okay ... so I can't beat you."
    "Better look next time Ragnor, maybe in a couple of more years ... Yes?" With that Jacobi turned and walked out of the circle.
    All the other angels could feel the seething anger of Ragnor.

"But you forget, master. I am good enough! And I am also better!"

So just as Jacobi turned around to look, Ragnor leapt upon the much older, wiser angel.

"Arrrrgghhh" screamed Jacobi in pain. Ragnor had both hands over Jacobi's face, pressing his right thumb into his left eye. There was a resounding pop, and Jacobi's eye was no more.

"Be gone you heathen! You are banished by law and the law of the Elders.

The regretful Ragnor turned and flew and was but a tiny speck on the horizon. Then he just disappeared, never to be spoken about in the scriptures ever again.

(That was his punishment, as well as never to be what he so longed for: A fully fledged angel).

Hell Again

"Have you or have you not come to seek out an agreement?

"I am sick of the hierarchy and the rules and boundaries they put on combat!" He spat.

"Well, shall I show you what being down here is like. Shall I?"

"Yes. Please do, master."

"Dip your finger into the molten lava and you shall see the power of the underworld."

Ragnor was a little apprehensive as he did this, but not scared. Straightaway the molten lava travelled up his finger, which turned his hand into a talon and his arm bulkier than it had ever been before.

"What is happening to me?"

"You shall see. Ragnor, you shall be an outlet of my destruction and you will do as you are bid. Do you understand?"

"Yes, master!"

"Now go to the muddy pool and see what you have become."

Ragnor peered into the muddy pool and his reflection was as hideous as it was grotesque.

"Master, what have you done to me?"

"Silence. I have made you more powerful and fuller than you ever were before. I have also made you ten times stronger, a hundred times quicker and a thousand times more deadlier."

Back at the graveyard

Asillian stacked pew after pew and barred the door so no dead could get in.

"Stand back just in case it doesn't hold."

Rowan was scared now and replied, "What if they get in and you can't protect us?"

"Always have faith Rowan, It will get you far."

"So Asillian, what do we do?" cried Amelia.

"Well, they can't cross the threshold unless we invite them in. So we are all good at that end."

Moaning and groaning could be what was to be rain and thunder ... This was after an hour, in the church. Amelia was beginning to get scared, but when she glanced at Asillian her fears went away immediately. She kept thinking about what Asillian had said to her about angels having an alluring smell and how they couldn't control it.

Amelia looked around the inside of the church and spotted a stairwell leading down to a wooden door. She cried out, "There's a doorway here."

Rowan could not believe his eyes. She was right, there was a door!

A bang could be heard at the front of the church.

"Hurry, they're nearly through, we need to leave!"

Outside

"*He* will be pleased to know I'm going to drag your carcass all the way back to Hell," hissed Ragnor.

"Not a cat in hell's chance," retorted Jacobi.

As the two giants battled, Jacobi noticed that Ragnor's strength was increasing. The souls were coming from Hell and flowing into Bane.

"I don't know where your strength is coming from Ragnor, but I will destroy you!"

Ragnor boasted, "The new weapon my master gave me will end you Jacobi."

Racing through the sky Jacobi and Ragnor pitted wits and brawn. When Ragnor thought he was winning the bout, Jacobi unhooked a glass of holy water from his belt, and threw it at Ragnor.

It smashed over his arm melting and burning flesh straightaway.

Ragnor gave out an outlandish scream and backed away from Jacobi's reach.

"You see not so powerful after all!" said Jacobi.

I will return and when I do be ready!" spat Ragnor.

As the dead tried to get in Amelia and Rowan reached for the handle of the door.

"What is this you've splashed on me ex-master?"

"Pure holy water, how's it feel?"

Then came a booming voice from nowhere.

"Ragnor, you must return at once. He commanded."

Ragnor did and in a puff of purple and orange haze he was gone.

Boil, the little shit, zipped in and out of where the dead were supposed to be!

"You cannot hide in there forever you know? The dead will get in eventually!" he hissed, "so why don't you just give me the freer stone?" He slathered with his devilish tongue.

"Asillian," shouted Jacobi, "is there a back way out of there?"

"Yes," came the reply

"Jacobi, use some of your mind control and confuse most of the dead that there's no one in here!"

"I would but they have no thought process. They seem to be controlled by *Him*"

With that on his mind he spun his staff round and round counter-clockwise, creating a windmill of ferocious speed. The dead limbs flew everywhere, and they all began to fall to pieces!

As the groans became thuds and cracks, Amelia and Asillian were hoping and praying that the front door of the church would not explode into splinters. It did but when Amelia turned round to see if Rowan was there ... he wasn't!

"Oh no!" said Asillian fearing the worst. "I have a feeling he has betrayed your trust Amelia, but I am not certain."

The car's wheels screeched as Rowan sped out of the church and began down the country lanes with Boil in the back seat.

"Let me see it ... let me sseee!"

Rowan was cautious, "First, minion you have to promise me what your master promised me!"

"Yes ... you will live forever. Now give me the stone!"

Rowan reluctantly gave the freer stone to Boil.

"Yes, yes we have it now, master?" And now you have to do me one more favour, mortal!"

"Anything, name it?"

"Die"

At that exact moment Boil sunk his fangs into Rowan's hand and the car veered right and smashed straight into a tree. When Amelia and the two angels had caught up with the smash, there in the driver's side was Rowan, his neck pouring with blood.

"If you hurry we can still save him if you pull him out of that seat and I mean quickly," said the young angel.

"How?" said Amelia, after all the injury looked fatal.

Jacobi plucked a feather from one of his gigantic wings and laid it on Rowan's neck. Magically, the feather began to soak up and heal the gaping wound. It clotted with miraculous effort.

"Here," Jacobi said to Amelia giving her the smelling salts.

Rowan sat bolt upright immediately.

"Uurrghh, that was like smelling pure urine. Where am I and what happened?" he managed to utter.

Amelia was furious. "Why did you give the freer stone to that creature?" she asked.

"His master offered me eternal life!"

"But doesn't seeing angels show you that there is something after death, especially eternal life!" she said angrily.

"That conniving bastard. I'll sort *Him* when I see *Him*."

Asillian had to interrupt. "You do realise *He* is just a presence and not a person?"

"So I can't actually harm *Him*?"

"No. But as angels and God's right hand, me and Jacobi can!"

They have It

Boil scampered into the underground lava den, then the booming voice was there. "Do you have the stone, Boil?" "Yes, my master" and Ragnor made a fool of himself, in trying to kill his old master Jacobi.

"Ah, I see he used sacred holy water on you. I should have known he would use tactics like that. Anyway, you're back in what is nearly one piece and I see you kept Bane?"

"Yes, he seemed to like the task of duelling with him. Found it to be, what was the word ... sporting!"

"Ha, sporting. You have yet to see what real power Bane has. But now that we have what we need, we can open the channel between Earth and Hell."

"Brilliant master, but how long will it take?"

"As much time as it needed. Now Ragnor, redip your hand in the lava and it will heal."

Ragnor did so unhesitatingly. He brought his arm out of the lava and it was just as before.

"Wow, master, you are truly powerful," hissed Boil.

"Our next stage of the plan is to resurrect Diabolos."
    "Who is he, my master?" said Ragnor.

"Just one of my many evildoers who will help you get the job done."
    "Now, leave me while I concentrate. Be gone!"

On the roadside

"We really need to get the stone back, it's imperative that we do," remarked Asillian.

"But how and who is going to sneak into Hell to get it back?" said Amelia.

Rowan then perked up, "I know of someone!"

"Like the fuck we can trust you, Rowan!" Asillian cursed.
    "Well, I do suppose in saving my life I owe you all don't I?"
    "Yes, you could say that for definite," replied Amelia.

So they trooped across town to the local gambling spots. It was night by this time and the two angels had rucksacks on to cover their wings, so didn't look out of place. They turned a corner and all of them could see the neon sign outside which read CLANSEY'S in purple.

"This the place?" asked Asillian sceptically.

"Yea, but when we get in let me do the talking," said Rowan.

"Lead the way," ushered Asillian.

Rowan beat on the huge, heavy steel door. A rectangular shutter opened and Rowan showed the bouncer his tattoo on his wrist. Amelia had caught sight of it and realised she had never seen Rowan with that tattoo before.

"Who are those two?" questioned the bouncer.

"Out of towners eager to spend some money."

The shutter closed and then there was the screech of bolts being released and the door swung open. Immediately smoke filled all of their noses, and quiet music could be heard. Foreign voices could also be heard as there was horse racing on TV, and people betting on rooster fighting.

"What kind of place is this?" said Amelia shocked.

"Don't worry, Amelia. Most of the people in here are gamblers, that's all," said Rowan. "Stick with me and you'll be all right."

As they passed the roulette wheel, Asillian spotted a huge bulk of a man, who seemed to acknowledge Rowan. The only reason Asillian thought this was because the huge man smiled broadly at him.

"Well, well, have you come back to lose some more money Rowan?"

"No, Skinflint. I'm looking for Pick Quick. If you've seen her. I need a favour."

Pick Quick

"Well for that information I'll need a quick sporting bet from you."

"OK, I'll have the cock on the right, you're on the left," remarked Rowan.

Hushed chatter spread around the room; the cocks were about to fight.

"Fingers crossed," said Amelia to the three of them. The two cockerels stepped around each other aggressively. Then in a space of what was a millisecond they were at each other's throats, with razor blades flying.

"I can't watch this," said Amelia, "it's horrific." She turned away in disgust. After what seemed like an age there was no noise. Amelia turned around and saw that one cockerel was still standing. The other was lifeless twitching on the floor.

"It seems you won the wager," said Skinflint to Rowan.

"You keep up your end then," said Rowan.

"She's in the back playing cards, you'll never get her out of there."

"Why ever not?" asked Rowan.

"She's winning," came the reply.

As the group came into the dimly lit room they noticed a very small figure waiting to be dealt her hand. She had unruly hair. It was as if she'd stuck her finger into an open socket, because it was that frizzy.

"Stick!" came the female's voice.

The dealer turned his cards over showing nineteen.

"Nineteen," said the dealer.

The petite female figure turned her cards over to show an excellent twenty-one!

Light applause went around the room.

Rowan tapped the female on the shoulder gently. She turned around.

"Rowan!" she said surprised.

"Pick Quick," he said nodding to her. Then they hugged.

Pick Quick looked at Amelia and the two angels ... "Who's the rabble?" She pointed.

"Just friends," commented Rowan.

Pick Quick was a master thief who knew all the above hand and below handed techniques to robbing and stealing anything she desired. She wore a faded denim jacket and slim fitting white jeans which had pockets and openings all over.

Asillian was sceptical when it came to trusting this woman, but he had second thoughts, knowing that Rowan had deceived them once and he might do it again unless he had learned from his near death experience.

The team acquainted Pick Quick with all the happenings, from Ragnor, *Him* and the freer stone.

"Holy shit! No way are you two angels. That's inconceivable! Prove it!"

Amelia nodded to Jacobi and Asillian and with that they burst out of the backpacks that were hiding their wings.

"Jesus, you really are angels!"

Suddenly Pick Quick was full of questions.

"That's amazing ... can you fly? ... how many of you are there? ... does Heaven exist?"

"Yes, we can fly. They are many of us. And yes, Heaven does exist," replied Asillian.

"So do you think it can be done?"

"I'm not sure but if you give me a little time I think we can work something out. We'll need Tull's help if we're going to do this right. Do you agree, Asillian?"

Asillian nodded in agreement then they left for Tull's place.

A mouse!

Tull had just finished some backbreaking work as he saw five figures coming towards his place.

He shape shifted into a mouse and hid quickly in the barn. He didn't feel like meeting the two angels and the friends that they were with, just then. So he just listened quietly.

"Where are you my old friend? It's an emergency and I wouldn't be here if it weren't. If you are there and you can hear me. I'll let you know this. They have the ring and are near to completing their task. So if you are there … please, we need you to be of assistance one more time."

The quintet heard a squeak and a scratching then suddenly a haystack burst into a heap revealing Tull, knackers and penis swinging about everywhere.

Amelia and Pick Quick averted their eyes.

"Tull, cover yourself up. They've never seen a shape shifter before."

"Oh, my apologies Jacobi, didn't realise. And what's this that you've brought more trouble my way?

"Two females and a male. Whatever is up with you?"

"Like I said they have the ring and they're going to try and use it to open a portal from Hell to Earth and from Earth to Heaven! Will you not help us?"

"On my life I will, I will do all I can to protect these people and stop evil rising once again."

Tull suggested that everyone except Asillian and Jacobi, should get a weapon from the barn. As the three sifted through the trash that was in the barnyard, Pick Quick looked about and chose a devil-like pitchfork. It was old and rusty but it would do the job. A pair of shears took the fancy of Rowan, and as for Amelia, it was a good old gardening hoe.

"Even though you've got these you wouldn't mind staying out of danger would you even though it'll be everywhere?"

"No," the three said in unison.

"Okay, so where to now?" asked Asillian.

Jacobi pulled out the magic map that would lead them to their next destination. The pair of angel wings glided across the page and settled on the crossroads. There was also a glyph that had a pair of red wings over the crossroads.

"I bet that means Ragnor's there," Amelia said angrily. "Oh yeah and that fucking imp creature." She cursed, which wasn't like her at all.

The crossroads

The landscape for the crossroads was different from anything you've ever imagined. A mixture of Heaven, Hell and Earth all dotted about the place. You would see a tree growing then black decaying bushes and dying flowers.

Or on the other hand a rainbow and then at the end a cesspit like no other.

The sextet which was now five waited behind to hear from Pick Quick about what was going on.

No one was there or at least that's what they thought until they saw Boil scamper slowly across the terrain.

Pick Quick sprang into action making sure she was keeping tabs on Boil. The quintet which was now four waited behind to hear from Pick Quick what was going off.

She had followed Boil behind a building and there she saw the huge imposing figure of Ragnor for the first time. She gasped and had to put her hand over her mouth, to stop herself from making a noise or being found out. To her grotesque astonishment she also saw another creature there.

It had a skull for a head and six arachnid legs with each looking as deadly as the other.

She noticed Ragnor had the ring on his finger and didn't look like he was going to let it go of it anytime soon.

Pick Quick listened to what they had to say then relayed it back to the group.

"So they're waiting for tonight, when the full moon will be out," mused Jacobi.

"We could attack now Wise one, and catch them off guard," said Asillian.

"No, two hours before midnight should be our window," interjected Tull. "That's when I'm at my most lethal. As you know Jacobi I draw most of my power from the moon."

"Yes, so just before midnight that's when we shall strike!"

The team waited with bated breath to see what the evildoers would do next. They lit a huge fire and began chanting incantations around it.

So the party was well underway ... demons of all types could be seen, slithering and scampering around. The larger of the demons just watched and were waiting for the full moon.

"If Ragnor has the ring we need somebody as a disguise or a doppelganger, such as Boil," said Rowan.

"Guess it's going to have to be you Pick Quick."

"Okay, okay but if I get into any trouble or danger you guys will protect me, won't you?"

"Of course, no doubt," said the two hulking great angels.

"Yes and I'll get them with this," Amelia said shaking the gardening hoe, comically in the air.

Jacobi and Asillian uttered a few of their own incantations from a book they'd studied before called 'The lesser evil.'

And Pick Quick turned into an exact copy of Boil!

"So while you're creating a distraction, I'll get the stone off Ragnor. Okay?"

"Sounds good," Amelia said.

Asillian came round one side of the building. Surprisingly, he wasn't noticed. Pick Quick did what she did best and blended in.

She'd got close then Asillian had been spotted. Pick Quick grabbed Boil and dragged him silently off to the side knocking him out with her weapon.

She then shimmied beside Ragnor, saying, "Hurry, master what if he obtains the ring?"

"That's why I'm going to give it to you Boil."

Diabolos

Just as Ragnor was about to take the ring off, and give it to Pick Quick the arachnid type looking demon interrupted.

"You give that to her and I'll kill you my fucking self," it said. "Can you not see through that ridiculous white magic bullshit and see that ... *that* is an impostor?

The skull-headed bony-featured arachnid-type demon, put its hands together and Pick Quick's disguise melted away.

"Damn you," said Asillian. "Who are you?"

"I am Diabolos, the Death Dealer! Who are you?"

"Well, you don't get to ask that question ... but just know that I am your end! I'm your Death Dealer."

"Go!" shouted Asillian as he drew his katana, and prepared for combat.

Asillian attacked first in a higher arch than usual. This caught Diabolos off guard but he easily defended the attacks by parrying his arachnid legs.

Ragnor watched on and flicked Pick Quick to one side with ease.

Jacobi sprang into action, leaping at least seven to eight metres in his stride. He hit Ragnor on the head with his staff, which dazed him for a few precious seconds.

"Unleash hell, my minions," cried Ragnor.

With that all the horrible and disgusting looking demons rushed forward, careering into the six figures with extreme intensity.

Rowan caught one of them in his shears hacking it in half. Amelia fended off two of the brutes with her gardening hoe. She gripped it and hung on for dear life. It was Tull's turn now.

His bones cracked and his skin tightened turning a jet black colour; he had morphed into a huge rhinoceros.

"Who wants a piece?" he said as he charged down a massive group of scourges, that looked ever advancing.

The six lone figures were giving it their all, but the ever advancing waves just kept coming.

"Oh God, if this is my end please let it be swift," Asillian prayed. They all did. Then just as all hope was lost a huge droning horn sounded and the skies lit up with sunshine. Winged angels started to descend from the heavens atop of even larger winged beasts.

They had been heard ... Yes, somehow they had been heard.

This gave new and unending hope to the six of them and their cause. Asillian fended of all of the so-called Death Dealer's attacks like water off a duck's back.

"Ha! Give it up now and I won't kill you Diabolos," promised Asillian.

"Never. You can't better me. I have four times the amount of appendages you have plus you're tiring."

"Oh yeah, try this on for size."

Asillian came with a flurry of attacks, spun, sidestepped the arachnid-type monstrosity and sliced clean through the demon's back cleaving him from head to toe.

Diabolos stood there for several seconds then slithered to the ground in two, green, gooey parts.

Wise Words

Amelia was absolutely terrified but she heard a voice say, "You are the chosen one my love and the scroll is the key. Forget about the stone now!"

Amelia was in no doubt whose voice it was. it had to be her mother or father. So she shouted this information at Jacobi as he had the map.

"It has a message written on the back that only I can read!"

Just as things were looking up, the full moon could be seen appearing from behind a sinister cloud.

"Now!" screamed Ragnor.

Just then the minions and demons overpowered the masses of angels for a brief second or so.

This meant that Ragnor could utter a few words while he resurrected his master.

"Exvictus!" whispered Ragnor.

Slowly but surely the ground started to shake violently. Then all the concrete cracked behind the battle and a massive smoky ... what can only be described as a gaseous monster came into view.

Then ...

Ragnor, thank you for resurrecting me!

"Anything, master. It is your will," replied Ragnor with his head bowed.

"I'll take it from here."

The gaseous figure moved towards Ragnor entering his body through his dragon-like snout. Suddenly Ragnor grew in size eight metres, 20 metres, 40. Eventually he stopped at around 60 metres high, huge talons and fangs baring.

Jacobi sent Asillian a telepathic message to get everyone to safety apart from Tull. Asillian did as Jacobi told him and hid them with white magic.

"What now?" questioned Asillian.
    "This is where we make our stand. Tull, you change into something that can contest with him ... yes?"
    "Yes."
    With that, Tull shape-shifted into a giant and started grappling with the bigger Ragnor.
    "When I throw these cars at him you shoot out their petrol tanks. Okay?" asked Jacobi making sure Asillian knew the plan.
    "Got it!"

With that Jacobi heaved his first car sending it flying into *his* face.
    Asillian didn't shoot.
    "Shoot, damn you!" shouted Jacobi.
    "I can't, I'll hit Tull," he replied panicking.
    "Then use the curve, you fool."
    Jacobi hurled another at Lucifer. This time Asillian took a sharp breath in thought of only love and let fly.

Arrghh! You motherfucker. Come here!

He swung at Asillian with Bane. Asillian tried to fly out of the way but He sliced through his wings with the blade, severing them from his body.

Amelia came running, tears streaming down her face.

"Is he going to die Jacobi?" she asked.

"No ... but when angels lose their wings they become human."

Amelia stared longingly into Asillian's bright, blue eyes. Then kissed him passionately.

"I love you." she wept.

"And I you," he replied.

Rowan looked at Pick Quick with the bloody shears in his hands. "Should we?" he said.

"No," said Pick Quick rolling her eyes. "Are you insane? We don't have time for that!"

Biblical

Jacobi was wrestling mentally with the huge red, monstrosity trying to gain control of his mind. It was sort of working as Tull was winning the power struggle they were immersed in.

Jacobi launched the map towards Pick Quick. It landed at her feet.

"Quickly, Amelia. Open it up!"

Immediately after opening the map she could see the layout but no text. This confused her dramatically.

"It must be on the back," Rowan screamed. **Hurry**!"

Amelia turned the map over and immediately words started to form on the paper.

"What do I do?" she said not knowing.

"Just read it, I guess," said Rowan.

As the letters and words started to appear Amelia concentrated.

"Those who live in the shelter of the most high will find rest in the shadow of God.

This I declare. He alone is my refuge, my place of safety; he is God, and I trust in him."

"It's working, keep reading, Amelia!"

"He will shield me with his wings. He will shelter me with his feathers. His faithful promises are my armour and protection. Don't be afraid of the terrors of the night, nor fear the dangers of the day, nor dread the plague that stalks in darkness, nor the disaster that strikes now."

The vessel that was Ragnor screamed out in pain.

Still she kept reading: "Though a thousand fall at my side, though ten thousand are dying around me, these evils will not touch me. I will see it with my eyes, I will see how the wicked are punished.

If I make him my refuge, if I make the most high my shelter, no evil will conquer me, no plague will come near my dwelling.

For he orders his angels to protect me wherever I go.

They will hold me with their hands to keep me from striking my foot on a stone.

I will trample down lions and poisonous snakes; I will crush fierce lions and serpents under my feet!"

As Amelia glanced up she could see that Ragnor started to shrink inch by inch.

"Keep reading, Ami," said Pick Quick.

God says "I will rescue those who love me. I will protect those who trust in my name.

When they call on me, I will answer, I will be with them in trouble.

I will rescue them and honour them.

I will satisfy them with a long life and give them my salvation."

By this time Ragnor was a miniature size now no bigger than a hamster.

"Finish it!" Asillian said faintly.

"In God's name, be gone," screamed Amelia, and with that Ragnor exploded into a giant green snot ball.

The ring was left behind.

"Well, I'm glad that's over," said Asillian. "But how do we repair the seal?"

"Easy," Jacobi said, throwing the ring to Tull. "We give it to Tull and he'll melt it down and that will be that! Seal repaired."

Amelia smiled at Asillian, "I always had faith you know?"

"So did I, my love … so did I."

The End

Peter James Hutchinson was born in the Yorkshire city of Doncaster, a former mining centre, minster and market town in Northern England, in 1986. He attended Park Primary School in Wheatley from 1991 to 1997 before going on to college to study the performing arts – he achieved high grades in both drama and dance. The Freer's Stone, a work of visionary science fiction, is his first foray into the literary arts. When not writing, Peter enjoys going to the gym, swimming and poetry.

The publisher

*He who stops
getting better
stops being good.*

This is the motto of novum publishing, and our focus
is on finding new manuscripts, publishing them and
offering long-term support to the authors.
Our publishing house was founded in 1997, and since
then it has become THE expert for new authors and
has won numerous awards.

**Our editorial team will peruse each manuscript
within a few weeks free of charge and without
obligation.**

You will find more information about
novum publishing and our books on the internet:

w w w . n o v u m - p u b l i s h i n g . c o . u k